Voice of the Morning

"South Africa has a greater variety of tensions than any other country in the world. There are tensions between Whites and Asians, between Black and Asians, between White and Cape Colored, Afrikaner and British, between both Afrikaner, British and Black. Most of my life I have been conscious of this dark potential in the future of my native country. Wherever I went the sense of conflict grew, the feeling of loss sharpened. . . ."

(Laurens Van Der Post in "The Heart of the Hunter")

Voice of the Morning

"Winds of change are sweeping across Africa. . . ."
(Harold Macmillan, Prime Minister of Britain in 1960)

by
ALAN LIVINGSTONE WILSON
Author of *Tagati, Doctor in the Jungle, Doctor in a Dark Land*

ZONDERVAN PUBLISHING HOUSE
GRAND RAPIDS, MICHIGAN

VOICE OF THE MORNING

Grand Rapids, Michigan

Library of Congress Catalog Card Number: 68-22168

Printed in the United States of America

Voice of the Morning

GLOSSARY OF AFRICAN WORDS

Baas or *Bwana* – master
indaba – council
Kaffir – Arabic for "unbeliever"
kraal – group of huts or village
kya – one hut or home
Location – the African or native part of the city
lungeli – all right
Mfundisi – teacher or pastor
mompara – fool, monkey
muntu – a youth
Nkulunkulu – the Great-Great, God
piccannin – baby
sadsa – corn mush
sakabona – a greeting
sebenzi – work
simba – lion
skelm – rascal
slala gashl – farewell greeting
tagati – witchcraft
tsotsi – African hooligan; young gangster
Ujesu Kristu – Jesus Christ
Umlungu – hyena

1

FROM HIS VANTAGE POINT Jonah Umlungu could see "Goldie" – the city of Johannesburg as it is called by the African. His ebony face was wrinkled in a frown. For an instant he did not know whether he loved this White Man's city or despised it.

"There is nothing like it among our native *kraals*. There the *kyas* are made of boughs and straw. Here there are great buildings and no small huts," he said aloud.

The White Man's city was beginning to change in a kaleidoscopic fashion. Night comes quickly here – not only in the jungle, but in the city, too. "It is all like a witch doctor's vision to me. When I first came to Goldie, I stood and stared – like the impala when he sees his first man. Buildings so tall I got an ache in my neck as I try to see them all. And the cars – so many of them . . . big and small, noisy and smelly . . . I remember all this made my heart as water."

Jonah turned and continued. "But night in the White Man's city is the greatest wonder of all!" He gestured to the city behind him, now coming alive with neon. To his right Jonah could see the big word ESSO and the OLA from the Coca Cola sign. "I remember the pop sign. The big bottle always pours and never makes the glass to run over." And as if to verify his remark, he turned to see the giant neon bottle pour out its showers of gold into the glittering glass, in a fantasy of changing colors and shifting patterns.

"It is all too wonderful for me."

"But you haven't told me why you are in prison. . . ."

The voice rudely reversed Jonah's reverie. He turned to look at the older black man who sat on the bunk in the dark, dirty cell.

In the ten minutes the Reverend Gideon Mukalo had been in that lonely cubicle with Jonah he had watched the youth change from an arrogant, tough *tsotsi* to a tired, helpless boy. A twinge of pity and self-consciousness made the elder man stutter.

"I'm sorry, Jonah. I did not mean to sound so abrupt."

The youth tried for some of his former arrogance. "Why are

you so interested in why I'm here?" Then he added flatly, "Besides, you already know. . . ."

"I've told you, son. I am the chaplain – the African chaplain to this prison. I want to help you. And yes, I know the crime you are charged with. But I want to hear your story."

The chaplain's words were reassuring. Jonah wiped the sweat from his face on the sleeve of his shirt. Then he stared at the shirt for a brief moment before talking. His thoughts were moving faster than his tongue could frame them into words.

It is this shirt that put me in prison! His mind raced back to the time when he first donned the red shirt of the *tsotsis,* the wild gang running rampant in the night, baiting the White Policeman to chase them down back alleys and over fences.

During the conversational lull, Gideon's mind was also active. *Like so many of the young Zulus,* Mukalo thought as he watched the youth. *There are so many Blacks shut away in this prison, away from the bright lights of the city. They do not understand the White Man's laws – rules as winding and aimless as the paths that run over the Zululand hills. They understand the laws of the tribe – those ageless laws passed down from father to son – the fear of the witch doctor, the fear of the chief. They are afraid of the medicine man's magic powers. So,* Gideon mused, *they do not commit evil – not because they love righteousness, but because know the witch doctor will "smell them out" if they do wrong.*

But they will not stay in the kraals *and on the reserves. They rally to the lure of the big city which calls them with its excitement and glitter and wealth. So, off they go. On the Rand, in the city, they soon forget the simple ways of tribal life . . .* sadsa *bubbling in the three-legged iron pot, the smell of wood fires and roasting meat from a fresh hunt . . . the sound of wind sighing among the aloes.*

Gideon sighed. *No, they do not stay in the hills tending goats. Instead, they come to live among the smells and noise of the shanty-towns, living like the animals they penned at home, packed into one stuffy apartment room or ramshackle flat, so different from the airy* kya *at home. Yet the thrill of the city – the sight of the shining display of gadgets and guns in the White Man's stores makes them forget the ways of their forefathers in the hills. So they break many of the White Man's laws, and learn the hard way that it means loss of freedom and punishment.*

Gideon's eyes focused on the youth standing near him and he remembered why he was there.

The young prisoner seemed more trusting now. He looked intently at the chaplain. "Can you really help me? I don't think you can. Maybe . . . ."

As though to add to the youth's despair the older man said, "I understand you have no friends and no lawyer . . . and that your first court appearance is to be on Monday."

Jonah nodded slowly. His eyes were very red and now heavy with a layer of tears which he refused to let flow. "How did you know of me?"

The chaplain took an envelope from his pocket. It was marred and creased from much handling. He showed it to the youth.

"Your mother heard of your trouble and wrote me. It is strange. No news from you for many a moon, then, as though the talking drums have been busy, comes news from the Big City."

Gideon sat on the cot beside the youth while Jonah read the letter. It was unbearably hot in the tiny cell and Gideon took off his jacket and pith helmet. He wiped his wide brow with a huge handkerchief and spoke once more. "You must tell me all, son. You have done a great evil. It will go better for you if you confess and plead guilty. It could be that you will get off with what the White Man calls a 'life sentence.' "

Jonah sat upright as though stung. "But I did not kill the man! Did I not tell the White Police that . . . many times? They did not believe me and I can see that you do not either." He buried his head in his hands and Gideon thought he might be crying. The youth continued, his voice strained with emotion and muffled through his hands. "It is no use! All my life the Curse has followed me. I shall never throw it off. This is the worst luck it has brought me and . . . ." His voice trailed off into half sobs and muddled words Gideon couldn't quite comprehend. But the plaintive quality of his expression Gideon understood.

Outside the cell the white jailer was getting impatient. *The black preacher has been in there with the kid for fifteen minutes now,* he thought. *I'd better make him leave. Besides, he ought to forget about that no-good nigger. If it was up to me, every nigger that pulled a gun on a White Man* . . . and his thoughts continued, a collection of angry obscenities. He shifted his position slightly and hitched up the heavy gunbelt. His small hand found the handle of the big revolver and unconsciously gripped the gun. He felt vastly superior to these "Kaffirs" inside the cell. Finally he spoke. The words were not spoken in kindness or the flat business-like tones of one imparting information. His voice was full of condescension and hatred as he snarled through the bars, "C'mon, there. Talk if yer goin' to. I ain't givin' ya the night, I ain't. Jus' ten more minutes is what ya've got."

The hard voice prompted the two men inside the cell to resume their conversation. Gideon looked at the youth. His eyes softened. He, the Reverend Gideon Mukalo, African chaplain of the prison, was once a boy like this . . . in trouble with the White Man's law. *Perhaps Jonah is innocent,* he mused, *but a White Man has been killed. And someone will have to pay the penalty. There may have been others, but this one they have – and he is safely in their prison. He is their victim.*

"I will try and believe you, my son. But you must take the padlock off your heart and lips and tell me all. And what is this 'Curse' you speak of? I know our people are superstitious – I was once myself – but I learned to know God, the Great-Great, Nkulunkulu. I saw that He is stronger than all the devilishness that the Evil One lets loose on the land."

Jonah looked at the elder black. Gideon had a face he could trust, but since his early days Jonah had been betrayed every time he put confidence in someone. Always he would be betrayed. All men were his enemies. *But then,* he thought, *I must tell someone and I can lose nothing. All is already hopeless.* He sighed heavily and began.

"I came here from Amanzimtoti. I was not used to the ways of the Big City. I was very overwhelmed at it all – even as I told you. But the excitement and color did not last. I got in trouble . . . was in jail and out of jail much – mostly because I did not have enough of the 'passes' we Blacks must have. We must have ten, you know: one to tell the White Man who you are . . . where you come from . . . who your parents are . . . another to tell who you work for . . . another to give you permission to go out after sundown . . . and another to–––"

The chaplain raised his hand. "Yes, yes. I know!" He looked warily toward the door and reminded Jonah of the jailer just outside. He spoke just above a whisper. "We Africans have many burdens to bear. But we must be patient and not be carried away by the hot-headed ones. I know how hard it is . . . ." He paused briefly. The young man was listening attentively, so he continued. "I know how hard it is. All around us we see our fellow-nations gaining *Uhuru,** and throwing off the shackles of centuries. But we must

* Independence

go carefully. In this land the White Man has the money and the power. He has many soldiers, many police . . . many tanks, planes and guns. And we have our Zulu spears." The youth's face once again clouded with despair. So the chaplain said, "But it will change one day! We will have Uhuru. I believe the Great-Great . . . Nkulunkulu . . . will deliver us in His own good time. But go on with your story."

Jonah nodded and resumed his narrative. "I joined a gang called 'the Russians.' We wore shirts the color of the bush that flames on the veld – like the one I wear now. And we have hats that the White Man calls 'a fez.' We went out every night, looking for excitement. We would get the White Police to chase us. Sometimes we would run down alleys and knock over garbage pails. Other times we would sit on the benches in the park that say 'for whites only' until the policeman would chase us with his club and bad words. Sometimes . . . ." The youth looked down and his voice matched his expression. In low flat tones he muttered, "Sometimes we would steal things from outside the Jew's second-hand store."

Gideon nodded but said nothing. Jonah continued.

"But that night I did not know the gang was planning to rob the White Man's store on Rissik street. I thought it was just to be another night of fun and mischief . . . ." Jonah recalled the events of that night as though they were happening again at that moment . . . .

The gang was cautiously moving up the dark alley careful not to be seen by any of the Whites who would surely call the police. Jonah was excited. Every time they roamed the streets they would make noise and arouse the indignation of the White Man. He looked down the long dark alley at the scores of garbage cans gleaming in limited reflections of light. *This will be fun,* he thought. *We can run the length of the alley and make so much noise the Whites will think it is a war!*

Jonah had not been a *tsotsi* for long, but already his training in the art of mischief had him thinking of an escape route. That was the first law of the gang member. To get away. Jonah did not need to train for that. All his life he would plot an escape route from any situation in which he found himself. Tonight was no different. He saw a passageway running at right angles to the alley. *If trouble comes most likely the two ends of the alley will be blocked,* he reasoned. *I will head for that passageway and escape in the darkness.*

His thoughts were interrupted. The others had stopped at the tongue. You will understand some of the strange and terrible beliefs of our people?"

Gideon nodded. "Some still live in the dark night of devilish black magic."

"The demons had snatched three babies from my mother. The Wizard had told her someone must have cast an evil spell on her – jealous, no doubt, of the beauty of those *picannins* – so when she knew another one was coming she made my father take her to the Witch Doctor. She was desperate to have him cast a counter-spell so that the demons would not be able to seize yet another child. 'Take the fattest goat from the flock, my husband,' she said, 'and a big bag of mealie-meal. We must not spare of our possessions to make sure we have a son – a warrior to follow in your steps.'

"My father was not too pleased to have to give his best goat, or the bag of meal. The drought had been bad that year and food was scarce. But he knew that if he wanted a son to carry on his name he would have to make the sacrifice." A dark shadow came over the face of the prisoner as he thought of the dangers his mother had told him of.

"Knowing our customs, Mfundisi," he said, "you will understand that evil spirits lurk everywhere. They see us, but we do not see them." He looked fearfully around the cell. "They did their best to prevent my parents from getting that Strong Medicine which would defeat their purposes. My father entered the jungle, leading the goat on a string, my mother following, bent low with the weight of the meal. It had been sunny. Now the sky suddenly grew black. A flash of lightning was followed by a terrible clap of thunder. My mother shrieked. 'The tree! the tree!' There was a creaking and a cracking and my father pulled himself and the goat away just in time. An old dead tree fell right across their path!"

Jonah wiped the sweat from his brow with a trembling hand. "That was only the beginning. One trouble followed another. Malenzi, the leopard, sprang on the goat as it walked past a baobob tree. Muzaboka is cruel but brave. He struck it a mighty blow with his knobkerry and the big cat rushed away screeching. Old Bulungu, the crocodile, lurked by the river crossing and lashed out with his tail at my father's legs, but again Muzaboka's courage came to the rescue and they crossed in safety. Karanzi, the cheetah, and Nyoka, the cobra, both tried to fulfill the demon's purpose, but my mother's determination and my father's bravery triumphed and they reached the witch doctor Madadikto's *kraal* at last."

To Gideon the story was as much legend as fact but he did not say so.

Jonah rose in his excitement and paced the cell. Plainly he was living over again his mother's story. "You won't believe this. Old Madadikto gave my mother advice that was weird but full of wisdom."

"Yes, evil wisdom, no doubt——"

"He said the only way to defeat the evil spirits who had stolen my mother's other *piccannins* was to deceive them – by saying it around that the babe to be born was not human." His voice sank to a hissing sound. "It must be called 'Umlungu' – Hyena!"

He dropped onto the bench again and covered his face. The chaplain's impassive face was stern. "They were evil words," he said. "Madadikto just wanted to get a reward and keep his hold on your parents. No doubt the *piccannins* died of natural causes."

Jonah lifted his head. "But–but *I* was born! Nothing happened. I became a healthy child. Was the spell not broken? And Nomquba has had many children since. Was not Madadikto right?"

Gideon dabbed his face with the big white handkerchief. I see you are steeped in superstitious beliefs, my son," he said. "I suppose you feel that, being born with the name of the most despised animal in the jungle, your life is bound to be accursed? That everyone despises and hates you as they hate the hyena? How dark can my people be!" He shook his grey head sadly.

Jonah's cry was right from his heart. "Whatever it is, Mfundisi, I tell you my life has been spent under the Curse. Nothing will take it away!"

"Surely you learned better than that at the mission school, where most of our people go at one time or another?"

Jonah nodded. "The good Mfundisi, Beckwith, did visit our *kraal* when I was about ten," he said. "He tried to persuade my father to let me go to the school, but Muzaboka is a stubborn man. He hates the White Man's religion. He always said the spirit worship of his ancestors was the only way. This time he said something that made my heart almost stop. He said, 'Hyena' – he loved to call me that – 'Hyena is to help the Witch Doctor . . . to learn to be like him!'

"I decided to run away. Next morning early I ran in the direction of the mission – they called it 'Hosanna.' I was not sure where it was, but at last I found it. I was too early so I sat on a bench and waited. I was pleased with the white-washed buildings. One, I found out later, was the school, another the church, another the clinic. It was all wonderful to me. Then the Mfundisi came out of his house and saw me. I told him my story and he welcomed me to the school.

"My heart was singing for happiness. I put aside the fear of meeting Muzaboka that night. It was a heaven of delight to mingle with the other native chldren and to hear the word of the teacher, Mr. Malesela – a good man! The Mfundisi came in one time and smiled at me. My heart beat for joy. I vowed there and then I would not become a Wizard; I would be a teacher in the White Man's world. Then the thought of the Curse came like a blow, and I felt sad. But in the excitement of learning the meaning of those strange letters and figures I forgot. But, oh, the home-going!"

"Did not the Mfundisi go with you?" inquired Gideon.

"He was going to but a messenger came for him to go to see a sick man at a far *kraal,* and . . . I . . . I had to make my way home alone." He paused and wiped the beads of sweat from his forehead at the memory of his father's cruelty. "It was very bad. My mother tried to help me, but Muzaboka struck her so that she lay as one dead. I cried myself to sleep. Next day I was taken – dazed as I was from my father's beating – to the Evil One, Madadikto. His face made my heart turn to water, and I begged my father to take me home. He laughed and pushed me toward the Witch Doctor. So my training in the ways of spirit worship began. It was easy at first – simply gathering herbs for the strong medicine the Wizard used, for, as you know, some of the potions are good to heal the sick. But some are poisons, which poured into an aching ear can cause deafness forever; or rubbed into a wound——"

"Do not tell me. Of that I know," reproved the chaplain. "Go on! The time grows short."

"I was to stay with him for one moon, then go home for the same period and return. One day Madadikto went home with me. I wondered why. He conferred with Muzaboka when we got home and then summoned all members of the tribe. My heart sank. I saw by the preparations that a ceremony was to begin, and I was to be the victim!" The young prisoner shivered in the heat. "It was evil – very bad medicine. The Old Man lit a fire and danced around it in a frenzy until foam was on his lips and his screams became hoarse. Then he seized me, called for a chicken, slit its throat and poured the warm blood over my head while I struggled and screamed. He muttered evil words – the words of a spell. Then he made me drink something. I nearly choked, it was so vile. I tried to push it away but a few blows from my father's stick made me quiet. Old Madadikto then fastened a string of evil charms around my neck, saying that if I took them off the ground would open and swallow me up! I was weak with fear.

"As soon as it was light next day I ran again to the mission school. I was too early but the Mfundisi saw me as he came out of his *kya* and made me go in. He asked me the meaning of the 'necklace' and when I told him, before I could stop him, he had taken a pair of scissors and cut it off! I held my breath, expecting the ground to swallow me, but all was the same. I breathed again. Tears ran down my face and the *bwana* told me not to be afraid. He said he'd go back home with me, and he did. He spoke strong words to my father, but I knew from the look Muzaboka gave me no good would come of the visit.

"Again I was sent to the Medicine Man. More charms were put around my neck. Mfundisi, it was an evil life – one moon spent with the powers of darkness, the next in the paradise of 'Hosanna.' I longed to take the Ujesu Kristus the Mfundisi spoke of into my heart, but my burden was too great. He could not take it away. I was too mixed up. The Curse lay heavily upon me and I could find no cure." The prisoner bowed his head and continued.

"One dark night I overheard Muzaboka and the Wizard – Madadikto – talking in my father's hut. I should not have listened, but I was always fearful and suspicious for I knew I could expect nothing but evil all my days. As I listened to their talk my hair seemed to rise up and much cold ran down my back. *I was to be turned into a leopard!"*

The chaplain turned his head sharply and looked into the boy's eyes, but all he saw there was sincerity . . . and horror. "You know all about the 'leopard men,' Mfundisi? They meet in the jungle at dead of night, the witch doctor" – he trembled and looked fearfully around the cell – "casts a spell on them and . . . and . . . they . . . they become howling jungle cats! They fix steel claws onto their fingers, they scream like a leopard, and they race through forest howling. If they meet anyone they tear them with their sharp claws."

Gideon's eyes revealed the question that was welling up in his heart. "And your father was actually planning to have the Wizard evil-wish you into a leopard man? Why did he hate you so?"

Jonah shook his head slowly. "It is hard, Mfundisi. I can only think he looks upon me as he has done since my birth – as an animal. To him I *really am* a hyena!" His voice was choked with fear and despair. "I suppose he felt it wouldn't make much difference if I changed into a leopard. Perhaps he wanted to be rid of me! That's when I ran away to the Rand!"

The chaplain laid his hand on the lad's shoulder. "Do not despair, my friend. The Word tells us there is hope – hope for the hopeless. Be of good courage!"

He took a worn Bible from his pocket. "Here is a story from God's Book that is something like your own case. It might help you." He put on a pair of spectacles and read the story of a great chief who was alarmed at the invasion into his land of a mighty tribe. "So he called in his Witch Doctor, Balaam, to call down a curse on the intruders. But every time he tried to utter terrible words," explained the chaplain, "he found himself saying good things . . . *good things!* When the chief rebuked him for disobeying his commands, he said, 'How shall I curse whom God hath not cursed?'

"My friend," said Gideon, "remember that story, and those words about it – 'The Lord, thy God, turned the curse into a blessing.' Do you not think He is powerful enough to turn your so-called curse into one? All you lack is faith – faith that will make you feel that God is stronger than the Devil and all the evil demons he has at his command. Let us talk to the Great-Great God, to Nkulunkulu." The two knelt on the concrete floor – taking no notice of the rattling of the bars as the jailer shook them, or at his grumbling at the length of time the black man had stayed there.

When they rose, Gideon murmured, as though his mind were far away, some words from a hymn that Jonah had sung many times at the White Man's mission settlement:

"Where He displays His healing power,
Death and the Curse are known no more . . ."

And for a moment, hope – like the last spark of a dying camp fire– flickered in the heart of the lonely prisoner.

The jailer unlocked the tiny cell and allowed Gideon to leave. He muttered something about the fact that "next time I won't be so generous; it will be fifteen minutes only, not one minute more . . ."

The gray-haired chaplain was not listening to the white man's grumblings. He was thinking about the young man in the tiny cell he had just left. *How odd,* Gideon thought, *that these black men should find themselves caught in the worst of two worlds. The primitive superstition of the tribal life often makes early widows . . . and the White Man's city is no different. We Blacks are without friends and homes – even in our own land.* But he forced his thoughts to more positive things, like the cool night air which would greet him when he left.

As the footsteps of the two men died down in the corridor, Jonah's head sank with his heart. He flung himself on the hard rough bunk to sleep.

But sleep comes fitfully to prisoners.

Jonah thought about Gideon and the good bit of optimism he brought. His mind then quickly reverted to thoughts of the Curse. All his life Jonah had known the potency of the Curse. Now he was twenty. And this latest and hardest blow once again confirmed the reality of a Curse. He was accused of the unpardonable sin of South Africa – the slaying of a White Man by a Black Man.

He tried to take his mind off these things, to concentrate on the sounds of the city he heard from his cell window. A distant clock struck the hours . . . a faraway shout . . . a laugh . . . the noises of cars. How often these same sounds had lulled Jonah to sleep in his flat. Now they mocked him.

Jonah's mind focused on the judge. Would he wear the dreaded black cap he had heard of? Would the Curse, for him, ever turn into a blessing as Gideon predicted? Would he ever be able to throw off the stigma of being a hyena? No answer came to him – just a jumble of questions. But mercifully, sleep came.

2

THE REVEREND GIDEON MUKALO called again the next day. He was accompanied by a tall, thin African, with eyes that looked as though they had always viewed sadness. They stopped at the door of the cell when, through the bars, they saw Jonah already had a visitor. He was a White Man – a fat man with a white suit, and cold blue eyes. He stopped talking and looked with anger at the two Africans. "Yes?" His voice had a knife-edge to it. It was bad enough to be with one Black – the prospect of being with three was more than the fat man could take.

Gideon shuffled his feet and turned his helmet round in his hands. He sensed that the white man was not pleased to be interrupted. "I–this is Mr. Moses Mapomulo, a lawyer." At this a small mean smile came over the white man's face but his eyes did not laugh. "He–he is willing to defend the prisoner . . . ."

The visitor stopped him with a quick wave of the hand. "You can save yourselves the trouble! I have been appointed to defend Umlungu," he said. His voice was tired, like a man who does not want to speak but feels he must make the effort. "Not that it will do any good. This man is undoubtedly guilty and, of course, there can be but one outcome – the death sentence. However, a benevolent government makes provision for even a Black pauper to be defended, so the trial will be fair. You need not wait!"

Gideon looked at Moses and the two walked slowly away, but the chaplain called out to Jonah, "We shall come back soon!" The white lawyer's face was angry but he turned again to the prisoner and began to talk rapidly. To Jonah his words did not make sense. They were in Afrikaans, the tongue of the other white race of South Africa.

"I–do not–understand," faltered the prisoner.

The white man swore. "Must I draw a diagram?" he said, in his tired voice. "You must plead guilty, and it is possible – barely possible – that you might get off with a life sentence."

Jonah caught the word "guilty." He was afraid of this White Man. He seemed to know that this man had condemned and sentenced him already and that he was only acting on Jonah's behalf because some Big Baas had asked him to. He wondered whether he should tell the lawyer that he was not guilty. Would it make any difference? He waited for a small space in the river of words and when at last it came, he said, in a quiet voice, "I did not kill the man!"

The white man stopped as though he had been shot. His face was of one who had been deeply hurt and his laugh was not merry. "They all say that," he said. "You're guilty, all right. Our police do not make mistakes. They picked you up at the scene of the crime and you had no explanation of why you were there. Now listen! Monday's trial is a mere preliminary one. You'll be remanded until the Autumn Assizes, then a jury will be chosen and you'll receive a fair trial and be sentenced. All you have to do Monday is plead guilty, then you'll be sent back here to await the real trial. Is that clear?" To him it was just business – something to be got over with as soon as possible so that he could get back to his White clients. But to Jonah it was all like the tangle of thorns around the cattle *kraal*. He sat with sorrow and puzzlement on his face. It was of no use to say any more. He knew nothing. He, this White Lawyer, was steeped in the law; he knew all about it. Jonah remained silent.

"All I can say in your defense," went on the white man, "is to say you were led astray by a gang of *tsotsis,* and that you are fresh from the country and didn't know what you were doing. Not that it's much of a defense. I'm afraid the judge will be merciless. There's too much of this gangsterism going on."

He might as well have spoken in Chizezuro, for Jonah only understood one or two words in the avalanche that the man poured forth. The lawyer rose quickly, catching up his shiny black briefcase. Jonah rose too, to show respect to this White Bwana.

"Clean yourself up for Monday," said the man. "Get someone to bring you a clean shirt and throw away that ridiculous red one. It'll go against you to be seen like that. That marks you as a member of a gang, and the judge will pounce on you like – like a lion if you show up like that!" He was kind enough to repeat the directions in English when he saw Jonah did not comprehend, then he shouted for the jailer and went off without a farewell salute.

Jonah walked up and down in the small space. He felt more despairing than ever. To think that his life lay in the hands of this fat White Man with the cold eyes and the tired voice! And where would he get a clean shirt ? The man may as well have asked him to wear a tuxedo – like those worn by the really Big Bwana he had seen the night they peeped in the windows of the Empire Club. Sorrow welled up from the pit of his stomach but he forced it back. He would not surrender to the devil of despair. He would remember he belonged to the proud Zulu race. Had he lived a century ago he would have been one of a thousand plumed warriors, armed with sharp *assegai* and cow-hide shield, decorated with white and black slashes. Why should he let these White Men think he was a slave?

Again the harsh voice of the jailer sounded – "Only fifteen minutes!" Rattling keys clicked open the lock and Gideon and Moses entered.

It was good to look into the solemn eyes of Mr. Mapomulo and to feel the grip of his hand as the chaplain introduced him. The three sat awkwardly on the rough bunk.

"What did the lawyer say?" asked Mr. Mukalo. "Did he tell you to plead guilty?" Jonah nodded. Gideon looked at Mapomulo who nodded slowly. "I knew he would do that." The chaplain's voice was stronger than usual. He was angry. "To him it is nothing that an African should perish or spend the rest of his life behind walls. Did he not ask you what happened?"

Again the prisoner shook his head. Gideon's words came out in an angry torrent but the lawyer raised his hand, a smile on his face. "Do not worry, my friend," he said, and his voice was like the law, deep notes of the great standing violin that Jonah had heard in the park one warm night. Somehow it seemed to bring a warmth to his cold heart and a pulse to his blood. This man would prove to be his true friend. Gideon was a true friend, too, but this man knew the law. Mapomulo had conquered the many hard barriers that the White Man's law had placed in his way. He had gone to school in spite of many hardships and much ridicule on the part of the white students. He had even gained a scholarship so that he could study at Fort Hare, the college for Blacks. And he had his degree, even though the European people and officials made it almost impossible for him to put it to good use. Still he was not bitter. He knew something of the peace that the Reverend Gideon Mukalo often spoke of and he believed that, in good time, right would triumph in his sad land.

"It matters not what happens at this preliminary appearance," he went on. "This will show you something of the devious ways of the White Man's law. The White Man himself calls it 'red tape.' You will appear only to be sent back to prison; it is just to get your name on the list of defendants for the Fall Assizes and to collect evidence against you!" Again his slow smile lit up his face. "I see it is all a big puzzle to you. But do not let it worry you. Very few – even Whites – understand the processes of the law. And today, what with the Minister of Justice passing a new law that anyone can be 'detained' (as they call it) for ninety days without a trial because he is suspected of criticizing the government, you will be lucky to get any trial at all."

Gideon spoke up. "But what is going to become of our young friend? I believe we both feel he is innocent of the charge. He was foolish to run in company with these *tsotsis,* but it was done in ignorance. Was it not natural for Jonah to seek life and excitement after his years of misery? Not that I am excusing the lad, but to charge him with the killing is wrong and we must not let him pay for a wrong not his."

The lawyer's head bowed in assent, and again Jonah felt a kindling in his heart at the thought of these two staunch friends. He spoke with much hesitation about the clothing the white lawyer had mentioned, and Gideon said quickly that he had already arranged for clean garments to be given the lad.

"What is more, I am getting you shoes!" Jonah felt that this was more than he had ever dreamed of.

The lawyer placed the tips of his long supple fingers together and pursed his lips. "We must plan what action to take, my friends," he said. "It is plain that this man – Mr. Jasper Cloete – must not 'defend' you. But what can two poor Africans do against the power of the White Man?"

A thought flashed into Jonah's mind. "Oh, if Mfundisi Beckwith were here," he said, and his eye lit up with joy at the memory of the man who had helped him in Zululand.

Again Moses nodded and Gideon said, "Good!"

The lawyer added, "But we must get someone here who has more authority than your country parson."

Gideon stood up. "I know!" he exclaimed, his voice high with intensity. "If ever there is a man of God it is the Rector, Mr. Pendelton. If anyone can sway the officials of the court into letting you, Moses, defend Jonah – so that one of his own will be behind him – he will do it!"

"Shall we go to him together?" asked Mapomulo. So it was arranged. Gideon took Jonah's hand, and again he addressed a few words to the Great-Great, to Nkulunkulu – making Jonah feel that He was actually in that hot cell, as close to him as were his two friends. He felt that if he could have remained forever in the company of these good men the Curse and its power would fade out and leave him in peace.

The chaplain was at the prison early on Monday. "I have written to Mfundisi Beckwith," he said. "I have urged him in the name of the Great God he serves to try to come to the Rand to help one of his former pupils. I have told him to come as soon as he can, so that together we may stand by you and do what we can to lessen your sentence. Mr. Mapomulo–the lawyer–thinks you should turn 'King's evidence' – you should tell all you know about the others who were with you that night and who committed this terrible thing . . . ."

Jonah shook his head. "I could never inform on my friends," he said sadly, "even if I must die. Who knows? Perhaps they will come forward and confess to the deed."

The chaplain looked in amazement at the prisoner. To think he should be so ignorant of the way of mankind that he would believe that anyone would confess to save the innocent! He shook his head. "No, my boy! Your so-called friends are probably in some hideout by day and only come out at night. They will wait until the trouble dies down – until your trial is over – and only then will they breathe more easily!"

He handed Jonah a parcel which had all the things he needed. Inside were clothes, even a pair of strong shoes – not new, but good. They fit well and Jonah was glad to put them on. He tried to thank the chaplain but Gideon stopped the grateful words by lifting his hand, and they sat down together.

"We have been to Mr. Pendelton's house," said Gideon. "As I said, he is a good man. He does not mind being called a *Kaffir boetjie* – a friend of the Kaffirs – if he is able to help us. He says he knows the local justice official very well and will have a long talk with him. No doubt he has already seen him. When you go into the Box you must plead 'not guilty.' Do not let the fat lawyer, Cloete, stampede you into saying that bad word, 'guilty.' That would be very wrong. Remember, we are praying for you. It may be that this terrible night you are going through is the rope that will draw you back to God . . . ."

The jailer came with the keys. His face was like a stone and he rattled the keys in the lock with much noise. His voice was harsh as he said, "Come on, you! No funny stuff!" He held out the handcuffs and the cold steel clicked around the youth's wrists. "To make sure you don't escape."

The chaplain looked as though he would speak but he closed his lips tightly and went out, waiting until the jailer and his assistant, with Jonah between them, walked down the corridor. Then he followed behind.

Jonah walked like one in a dream. He knew he was just a plaything in the hands of forces stronger than he – a poor African. What could he do? Why bother to fight against what had to be? He did not know the saying of his brother Africans in Kenya: "Shauri ya Mungu" – "it is the will of the Great-Great" – but he was thinking along those lines. *It is fate that a man should be swept along like a twig in the rushing water of the torrent. All that happens to him will happen: he can do nothing to stop it. How useless for the chip to try to swim against the current!* These were some of the thoughts passing through Jonah's mind as he walked to the waiting van.

He did not see the rushing rows of brick houses or stores as the car hurried along, not because the window was small and high but because his mind was turned inward. He thought only of the fate that lay ahead of him. The young prisoner knew now that this trial was only – what was it the fat white lawyer had said? – a preliminary one. But it did not matter. His feelings seemed to be frozen like one who had spent the night in a cave on the hills. Nothing mattered. Only now and again the words of the chaplain seemed to flash in his mind like a firefly on a summer night – "turn the Curse into a Blessing; turn the Curse into a Blessing." Well, that would never happen. A White Man had been killed and someone must be the scapegoat. *And why not me? At least it will put an end to my life of misery.*

The police van jerked to a quick stop and Jonah was hustled inside the stone building. The courtroom was crowded. Many people had come to see the wretched *Kaffir* who had dared to draw a gun on a White Man! When Jonah came into the courtroom a sound like the buzzing of wild bees in the veld was heard. Jonah gave one quick look around him. The crowd made his heart go cold. To see so many White People with so much hate in their eyes . . . their pointing fingers . . . their hissing whispers . . . further added to his misery. Did not Mukalo say his "friends" would be hiding in the depths of the darkest cellar? Not so! For in that one quick look he had seen a familiar face in that part of the gallery where the Blacks were allowed. It was "General Tarzan," whose real name was Nathan Kapazuni. Where the leader was the others could not be far away. Yes, there they were. Jonah looked again and saw two or three of the other *tsotsis* by the side of Tarzan.

Jonah soon forgot. A man in front was reading something in a monotone voice. Then the magistrate came in and everyone stood. A lot of talk followed but the prisoner did not understand much of it. When the time came for Jonah to take the stand he was glad the Reverend Pendelton stood up – just as quickly as the fat lawyer – and asked permission to speak. The fat one, Mr. Jasper Cloete, looked as though he wanted to shout at the rector, but it seemed the judge knew Mr. Pendelton and his stern face did not become any sterner. He nodded. Mr. Cloete, after trying to stare down the minister, sat down.

Mr. Pendelton's words were too difficult and quick for Jonah to understand all, but he knew they were good words. He understood the word "guilty" and "not guilty" and he heard Mr. Cloete's name mentioned. He saw the parson pointing at him, at which Mr. Cloete's brows came together, and he looked as though he would like to have attacked the pastor.

"What do you plead?" asked the magistrate.

Jonah looked at the chaplain and Mr. Pendelton. They both

shook their heads. "Not guilty." His voice shook like the sound of pipes. But his friends nodded, smiling. He had won his first victory. It was soon over. A man they called the "prosecutor" asked the magistrate for a remand. Jonah wanted to thank his new friend for helping him in this first stage of the trial but he was hustled out the back way into the van. This time the handcuffs were not used. Instead, a guard sat with him while his assistant rode in the front. A crowd of angry White People milled around the van and Jonah was afraid. He heard obscenities being shouted and he knew they were meant for him. He caught other words like "Kill him!" which he could understand, and he felt more afraid when banging sounds came on the sides of the van.

But the driver quickly put the vehicle in motion and the voices grew dim in the distance. Jonah sat thinking of the trial. He suddenly remembered seeing Tarzan get up and leave his seat. Soon the others, one by one, had followed. He wondered a little why they left before the "show" was over – he felt it was a show for many of the White People, but not for him. He wondered if his friends were among the crowds shouting outside the van, but he thought not. They would go away and hide again. It was good of them to risk arrest by coming to his trial.

The van had come to the Western Township, a part where many Africans lived. They had to go through that district to get back to the jail. The van was slowing up for some reason – he saw the guard get up and peer out the small window and mutter something about those "stupid, dirty niggers." Jonah didn't hear all of his words but understood his tone. He wondered if the natives knew it was the police car and if they knew he was in it.

The door suddenly burst open and the jailer tried to draw the revolver he wore from its holster on his belt. But he could not get it quickly and, in a moment, Tarzan Kapazuni – lithe as a leopard – was on him. "Get out, Jonah!" he was yelling, while others crowding in the back of the van echoed the cry. Jonah sat like one in a dream, but a long black arm came in and sinewy fingers grasped his ankle and pulled him along the smooth metal floor. The other jailer on the front seat tried to get to the back to help his partner but the crowd deterred him, their wild shouts and laughter filling the air. Jonah felt himself being pushed and pulled into the midst of the sweating crowd. Then, suddenly, he was bundled into an old car and it moved swiftly but noisily along the street and skidded round a corner. He heard the sound of shots, then the noise died away and they were alone.

The car veered around the next corner, again at the next and to the left at the next road. In and out they rushed and Jonah knew that they were doing it to keep anyone from following.

Fear pressed down on him like a heavy weight and set his whole body trembling. What was this madness? If he had been in a pit before this was much deeper! Why had his "friends" made this attempt to snatch him from the White Man's law? It could never succeed. They would pursue him to the ends of the earth and his last fate would be worse than the first. He could only gasp, "Why? oh, why?" to his noisy, laughing "rescuers." "General Tarzan" had managed to escape the reach of the guard in the van and clamber aboard while the car was moving. He was rejoicing that they had all managed to thwart the White Police. To them it was simply another reckless escapade, only a little more crazy than baiting the police as they had done so many times before.

They had now come to the narrow, smelly streets of one of Goldie's slums, where many thousands of Africans live in crowded rooms. "Get down to the floor," ordered the "General," and he pushed Jonah's head until it was below the seat and out of sight of the scores of black boys and girls thronging the streets, just home from school at noonday.

Up a narrow lane the car turned, then turned again and at last came to a shed that seemed to hold itself together by a miracle. One of the riders leaped out and opened the doors, the car moved in, and the doors were shut again.

"Here we stay until night," said the "General," "and then we take you to Nathaniel Kwanda."

"Who is he?"

They laughed at Jonah's ignorance. "You do not know the great Kwanda? He is many things. For one, he is editor of *Africa Speaks* – the only paper that tells the truth about us Africans. Yes, he alone puts our case before the people." This was another voice – that of Baswana.

"Kwanda is also head of the union," said Nahum. "I know he will have some useful work for you to do – for a man he has rescued from death and the prison."

"Then he was behind this rescue?" Jonah's voice was thin. He was more afraid than ever. It came to him now that he had heard of this man Kwanda. He had heard that he seemed to have much money, although the paper was not rich. The White Man would not advertise in it because it said many hard things about the Whites.

Jonah had heard that the money came from the Communists. Mfundisi Beckwith had warned him, back in the *kraal,* that these Red agents from overseas were always around when trouble was afoot. They knew the Africans were furious about their downtrodden state and they liked to pour oil on the flames and speak cunning words about how cruel the White Man was, how unjust. That led to blood being shed and strikes getting more violent. But all this, the Communists told them, would lead to *Uhuru,* independence – that wonderful thing all Africa was looking for, *Freedom!* It did not take much to stir up hatred against the White Man for every African wanted to feel free in his own country. Every Black Man wanted to have a go at making the laws. And every African wanted that privilege the White Man called "voting." Why should only the White Man have the fun of marking a small "x" on a little piece of paper at election time, while the Blacks looked on in envy and wonder? It was not right! *So,* thought Jonah, *the Reds have only to whisper the word Uhuru into our ears and we go mad and want to kill . . . to smash . . . to shout . . . to riot . . . to hate.*

Tarzan and Baswana got out of the car. "You must hide here until tonight," said Kapazuni, with his reckless laugh. "No one must see you here or else it's . . . ." He drew his hand in a slashing gesture across his throat. Jonah almost wished himself back in his cell. At least he was safe there. "We will bring you food. Tonight we take you to the Big Baas, Mr. Kwanda! You keep very, very still, or else . . . ." Again he punctuated the statement with a motion.

The door creaked closed. Jonah was left in darkness with the prospect of many hours imprisonment. He was hot and found it hard to swallow. *I have escaped from the White Man's prison but the whole of Goldie's mighty police force will be hunting me. Surely the Curse is working – bringing evil upon me worse than ever!* He tried very hard to pray but the words would not come. All he could manage was a weak stammer, "Nkulunkulu! Nkulunkulu!" Somehow even that seemed to bring a lull to the storm within him.

The door creaked again and his heart jumped. A tall, slim figure came in silently. It was a girl! She groped her way to the car, stopped, looked inside, and thrust through the open window a half loaf of bread. Jonah took it and laid it on the dirty, lumpy back seat. Then the girl handed him a tin cup. "Drink," she said in a voice that was low and sweet.

"Thank you," Jonah sighed, and sipped the native beer.

The girl stood there looking at the bedraggled youth, seeing past the torn clothes and sweat-covered face. She saw a good man under the shell of the prisoner exterior and her eyes revealed her concern.

For a brief moment they said nothing, just looked intently into each other's eyes. Finally Jonah broke the spell. "Who . . . who are you?" he managed to stammer.

"I . . . I am Miriam. I was sent to you from the 'General' to give you food. Are . . . are you in trouble?"

Jonah nodded that indeed he was in trouble. Sore trouble. He slowly got out of the car and stood beside the young girl. Her grace and fragrant presence were a welcome contrast to the presence of the gang members. He told her, briefly, of his situation. Then he asked, "You don't believe I am guilty, do you?"

Miriam looked away avoiding his face and searching eyes. Then she looked directly at him. Again their eyes met. "I do not think you would do it," she said simply.

There was something, unidentified between the two. Whatever it was it caused an instant affection. It was Jonah who put the feeling into words.

"You are very kind."

Miriam did not reply. Both were self-conscious now and Jonah took the conversation back to where it had stopped. "You are right. I did not kill the man. And I did not want to escape," he added with excitement in his voice. "I have a good man to defend me. I think he could get me off from hanging!"

The girl looked nervously at the door. "I must not stay. The 'General' will be angry. He is going to take you to Mr. Kwanda as soon as the sun goes down." Miriam paused. She did not like to think of the fact that she would never see this man again. She liked him . . .

Jonah spoke swiftly. "They say Kwanda will make me work for him. But I do not want to be mixed up in this thing. It is evil. The Communists———"

Miriam lifted a hand. "Shhhh-h. I know!" she said softly. "But do not mention the word. The White Man's government would shut away anyone who belongs to Communists. But you must do as they say. You have no other way . . . ." Her voice trailed off as Miriam secretly wished there was an alternate way.

Jonah leaned closer. If only he could get word to the chaplain and to Mr. Mapomulo – and maybe through them to Mr. Beckwith. "Would you try to get word to Mr. Mapomulo, the lawyer? If you could tell him I had nothing to do with this madness maybe he could do something."

The girl looked fearful. "If they find out I am as one dead."

Jonah sank back onto the car seat in despair.

"But I will try," she smiled. "I am not a bad girl. I work for Mr. Kwanda . . . in his office. I do not like him or his ways but I must have a job———"

Jonah nodded. That she should make such an effort at such a risk encouraged the young prisoner. His heart reached out in a quiet communication only the two of them understood.

She put her hand on his and squeezed it lightly. "I must go now."

Jonah felt an odd twinge – the pleasure of her touch and the sadness of her leaving.

The door opened and creaked shut, and he sat back on the bumpy back seat, his mind full of rushing thoughts. This girl coming into his life – so unexpected. To find an angel in this place of iniquity was a miracle. He had had nothing to do with girls in his home village. They treated him like the men did – with contempt. He was "Umlungu" – Hyena – to them. He was the Accursed One, a youth to be laughed at, spat upon, teased, made to do the menial tasks. But this girl had treated him with respect. Her eyes – he could see them still – looked full into his with a look that thrilled him. She had not laughed at him. She seemed to feel sorry for him. *And – and, she has half-promised to speak of my fate to my friends! Now, even if I do have to go through with their evil schemes, I will not mind so much. They will know I am acting against my will. They will pray for me!*

Exhausted from the day's rush and worry Jonah ate a little bread, then lay down on the rough seat and slept.

3

JONAH WOKE WITH A START. It was as dark as the jungle in the garage but the door was creaking and whispers came to him. He heard the voice of Tarzan. "It is me, Hyena – Tarzan. Keep quiet! The White Man's police have been swarming over the district. Good thing we hid you in here. They questioned Mr. Kwanda but he is very crafty. He did not give you away. He put them on a false trail!" His coarse laugh rang out, breaking his own rule of silence. But Tarzan lived for the excitement of risks. "Come. We go see Mr. Kwanda."

Jonah's throat felt dry again and he felt weak. "I . . . do not want to see this man!"

Another laugh, this time with curses. "He does not want to see the man! Ha!" He mocked Jonah's voice. The car door swung open and Tarzan's hand closed on Jonah's wrist like a vise and he was dragged out.

"All right, I'll go. I'll go!" Jonah cried, and he meekly accompanied the "General" across a lane, through a rickety gate in a board fence, over a rubbish pile of rusty tin-cans, into a brick building. It seemed many years old. In the background a hum made the building vibrate. To Jonah it sounded strange. Kapazuni laughed again.

"That's the printing press," he said. "Running off our own paper – *Africa Speaks*. Come! Up here!" Tarzan led the way up a narrow staircase, past a big room where the hum turned into a roar and black men shouted at one another as they staggered about with great arms-full of papers. They continued up the winding stair until they came to a door marked OFFICE. The door was closed. Tarzan knocked. Jonah couldn't hear the words from inside but they must have been "Come in," for Tarzan opened the door. Inside a man sat at a desk – obviously the important one named Kwanda. Kwanda was a black man whose big round head was shiny and whose neck was like a bull's. Jonah saw only his back and shiny head. Without turning the man spoke sharply.

"Sit!" Jonah sat down on a wooden chair, still nervous. Another man sat near the desk – an African in a splendid White Man's suit, bright blue, a white shirt with a big collar and a yellow tie with matching "puff" handkerchief. Clouds of smoke from his cigar filled the room. His bony hand rested on the handle of a native walking stick. He stared at Jonah and arrogantly blew smoke in his face. Finally Kwanda swung round in his chair.

"You go!" His voice was like the machine guns of the White Man's soldiers – sharp and quick. His eyes seemed to bore past Jonah and rested on Kapazuni, who with a "Lungeli, Baas!" ("All right, sir!") turned and went out.

Nathaniel Kwanda looked a long time at the prisoner until Jonah felt his stomach churn within him. Without a word the fat one picked up a paper from his desk. Big black letters stood out across the top. Jonah had seen the Johannesburg Star – he had even tried selling a few copies but the Curse had worked again (he had had his money stolen and the White Baas had fired him). He had learned to read at the mission school. The words on the paper were like a fist smashing him. Jonah read: ACCUSED MURDERER ESCAPES CUSTODY. The thin man with the cigar laughed; it was not a laugh good to hear.

"That's you, boy!" he grinned, showing gold in his teeth. Jonah fidgeted more than before. He knew why this man – the Big Baas, he who made even the Whites tremble – had shown him the paper. It was to show him his own hopelessness. He was a marked man. The Curse. Every man's hand was against him. He had broken away from the White Man's grasp. He had made fools of the White Police. They would put every power they had to work to get this "insolent Kaffir" who had not only dared to attack a White Man but who had the nerve to break loose! Jonah could imagine their anger and their fury in resolving to re-capture him.

The prisoner threw his hands up in a futile gesture. "What – what can I do? I did not want to–––"

"Stop!" Kwanda's face was full of anger. "We get you out of the hangman's noose and you keep us up 'til the middle of the night; and then you say you do not want us to help you. What kind of man are you?"

Jonah fell silent. What could he do? Wherever he turned he did the wrong thing.

"That's better! Now listen. You can – weak and stupid though you are – help us. You, Umlungu, can help the cause of the Black Man in Africa. I suppose even you have heard of *Uhuru?*" He stopped and Jonah nodded. "Well, it's coming to this land, too." He looked around; even *he* was afraid someone might hear him and he would be shut up forever. It was treason to talk of the Black Man wanting to be free in his own land. He lowered his voice but still spoke quick and sharp. "The White Man has the guns, tanks, planes. We have some weapons but not enough. Come closer, my friend!" He had given a strange inflection to that last word.

Jonah pulled his chair nearer. Kwanda leaned forward. "We need help from our brothers who have fought for their freedom," he said. "They have all the things the White Man has here. They must help us. They must liberate their brethren in slavery." Jonah said nothing. He wondered what was coming. Kwanda went on. "You know why I have chosen you to go to our brothers? Oh, don't think you are the only one." He grinned. "I have many secret agents. You could come across them in Rhodesia, Tanzania, Zambia, wherever you go. But———" He interrupted himself. "Stop shaking! I chose you because you cannot stay in this country. You are a fugitive. Your photo is in all the papers and police stations. Everyone will feel he is doing the government a favor to have you arrested!"

Jonah put his face into his hands and groaned. It was true. He was "as one dead." What was the use to struggle? The Curse had swallowed him up as surely as if he were already in Hell. "What–what do you want me to do?" His voice mirrored his despondency.

Kwanda hitched his chair nearer. "Tarzan will take you in the car as far as the border. He will stop far enough away so the guards will not see him and get suspicious. He will then take you to the river where I have a boat hidden – you will cross the river in the dark. The other side is Rhodesia. Watch out for the guards on both sides. They'll shoot on sight." His laugh was out of place here, but not out of character. Jonah did not like or trust him, but had no choice. "Once in Rhodesia you're on your own. You might be able to hitch a ride in a truck. Avoid the White Man's cars like the plague. Look for our own people – black truck drivers. Tarzan will give you new passes, new identification papers. You are no longer Jonah Umlungu. Don't forget! If you let them know who you are you are a dead man!"

He leaned back, his black, beady eyes fastened on Jonah's face. The calmness of despair had filled Jonah's soul. He was as helpless as the rock-rabbit when the python's eyes paralyzed it. He was the plaything of this power-mad maniac. All he could do was obey. Useless to think of escaping; he might get away from Kwanda, perhaps, but there was still the White Police to think of.

"You must keep out of sight as much as possible in Rhodesia. Fortunately the Matabele speak Zulu – they are an off-shoot of our race – and you will not be noticed too much; but you must make for Zambia . . . what they used to call" – his lip curled – "Northern Rhodesia. Ah, soon *all* the African nations will have their real native names again! There you must contact a man named Simba, the Lion. He will tell you what to do and where else to go."

Kwanda turned to his desk again and pulled something from a drawer. Jonah's eyes widened as he saw what it was – money! He had never seen so much before. Kwanda frowned. "I do not like to give you this money. You strike me as being very stupid. But you need money – you need to pay those who will hide you, so keep a strict account of it. I suppose you can put down figures? Some of this is Rhodesian currency, some Zambian. When this money is gone you'll have to make your own way."

He put the bills into a thick brown envelope and thrust it into Jonah's weak fingers. "Now, here's a word that will get you anywhere among our people and convince them you are one of us." He leaned forward again and hissed "Chaka!"

Jonah knew of Chaka, the tyrannical Zulu chief who had conquered a thousand other tribes and made himself a monster of power and cruelty. So Chaka was to be the hero of all Africa? He was to be the model on which Kwanda and other African leaders would carve themselves?

Kwanda was reading his thoughts. "Yes! Tyranny begets tyranny and the Whites will learn that by crushing the Blacks they are making us into merciless Chakas. Now, repeat that word!"

Jonah whispered "Chaka" softly and Kwanda seemed satisfied. The arrogant African strode to the door, pulled it open and shouted "Tarzan!" A voice replied from just outside.

"Off you go! All is ready!" commanded Kwanda. Jonah rose.

"Oh . . . before you go. You must know this man." Kwanda gestured over his shoulder to the man in the blue suit who had remained silent throughout the conversation. "He is my lieutenant. Umlungu, meet Mr. Judas Balatwa." The tall thin man did not acknowledge the introduction. Jonah dropped his hand when the one named Balatwa did not extend his.

Tarzan was there ready to escort the "escapee" to wherever it was he was going. Jonah did not dare to think about it. The two young men left the older pair and shut the office door.

As they left, Kwanda and the man with the cigar, Judas, laughed.

"That one. He was too scared to say much. You'll have him doing your work, that's for certain," grinned Balatwa.

Kwanda seemed irritated by the scene now that it had ended. "There was never any doubt about that. Now suppose you find something to do . . . . I have work that must be done. And get rid of that foul-smelling cigar."

"Lungeli, Baas!" The reply was the same as the lowly Tarzan's although Balatwa had not noticed. He left Kwanda grinning to himself about the similarity.

Kwanda sat back in his big chair and stared out the window behind his desk. *This Umlungu . . . frightened, but he'll be a good agent to have. He has nothing to lose . . . and a man in that kind of situation will perform the most bizarre feats for the Cause. Yes . . . he will be most helpful to me.* Kwanda was proud of his cunning. He had used much strategy in planning this "rescue" of the frightened youth. Even to the point of making Tarzan use his own car – just in case the plan was thwarted and the *tsotsis* captured. That way the police would not be able to trace the plan to him. Certainly Tarzan would not talk if captured. He was just as trusted as Judas Balatwa.

The big African turned slowly and smiled to himself. Then he reached for the stacks of *Africa Speaks* copy that needed his approval before the typesetter would get them. Kwanda began humming to himself, quietly.

4

THE "GENERAL" WAS ALLOWED to use Mr. Kwanda's auto for the journey north. Jonah was thankful for even this small mercy. He dreaded a long trip in the old car that had "rescued" him – it was doubtful that it would be able to make the trip and its seats were bumpy. He had the big back seat of the late model station wagon to himself; Kapazuni and Baswana sat in the front seat. Jonah was glad he would soon be forever free of them and their wild ways. Even to be a wanderer on the face of the earth was better than being mixed up in gang-fights, break-ins, even murder, with the inevitable White Man's police at the end. He sat huddled in his coat, soaked in his own thoughts. They were not wholly sad. The girl, Miriam, flitted in and out of them. Would he ever see her again? His journey would take him many moons. Would there be any return? He knew once he stepped inside South Africa again he would be seized and made to suffer for his awful crime of escaping custody, in addition to the punishment which faced him for a crime he did not commit.

And yet, somehow, a wild hope deep within his heart made him feel he would see her again. The Great-Great – who, the Mfundisi had said, would "turn the curse into a blessing" and who had already seemed to be near him in spite of his trouble – had some purpose in the meeting. True, he could see no flaw in the noose that seemed to be closing around him; yet, he believed that the light of hope would break through.

Tarzan knew plenty shortcuts for the car to slip out of the city. Jonah heard him say something about "road-blocks." That is why he took a very rough road leading through the scanty trees on the outskirts. "We join the main road when danger is past!" called out the driver, to explain the bumps and jolts. It must have been a good twenty miles later when Tarzan, with great caution, edged onto the main highway. "You see anything?" he asked Baswana.

"No! All clear!" And on they went.

The going was smoother and swifter. Jonah dozed. Suddenly the car slowed so quickly he shot forward onto the front seat. With a squeal of brakes the car stopped. Tarzan was swearing and muttering, and wrestling with the wheel. "Saw that road block just in time. Must go back to the last turn into the wood."

They swung around. "Hope they not see us!" whispered Baswana. "Quick, we hide in the woods!"

Jonah looked through the back window as the station wagon completed its turn. He could see in the distance a fence across the road and some people. They had lights. He thought he could see them pointing. "What you see, Hyena?" called Tarzan harshly.

"I think they see us," said Jonah.

The car completed its turn and squealed off into the darkness they had just left. Tarzan swung off the highway onto the dirt road with a lurch and a skid. He drove a few yards then plunged between some trees in an open space, turned off the lights and stopped. "We stay here in case they saw us! No noise, Hyena, or else———" Jonah knew the gesture Kapazuni had used, although he could not see it in the dark.

It was not long before the sound of a car was heard. It, too, slowed up with squealing noises and the headlights wheeled into the woods. "Still!" muttered Tarzan. "They will not see us!"

It was true. The big car with its flashing top-light roared down the dirt road. "Now we wait till they come back."

It was not long, perhaps half an hour. Then the car lights swayed into sight again, the car turned right and disappeared. "They go back to the road block. Good!" said Tarzan. He swung the car onto the dirt road again and continued through the trees, then turned north again. "This time we stay on back road until no more road block," he said. So they bumped and swayed over the bad road.

An hour later again the car edged out onto the highway. This time it seemed safe. They roared along at the car's maximum speed, with no more road blocks looming in their path. Jonah again fell asleep. It was not a good sleep. Many bad dreams – cruel, leering faces, came and went. There was Judas Balatwa, his gold teeth gleaming; the fat, bald head of Kwanda, the Assegai, his eyes like coals of fire; Simba, the Lion, whom he had never seen but was to meet – a great mouth, of lion's fangs, about to close on Jonah's head. He jerked awake, shivering. It was still night. The car zoomed on smoothly with Baswana snoring and Tarzan huddled behind the wheel, saying nothing. Jonah slept again, but he had more fantastic nightmares; it was a bad night for him.

5

THE REVEREND MICHAEL PENDELTON, Rector of All Saints, Johannesburg, opened the door of his manse. "Come in, my friends." His voice was grave. He had heard of the escape of the man he had tried to help. Now Jonah's two supporters were here for an *indaba.** The matter had become more serious than he wanted it to be.

Gideon Mukalo and Moses Mapomulo removed their hats and walked timidly into the front room. It was a house with a carpet and big padded chairs – the house of a White Mfundisi, one they seldom saw, and they trod with care. But Mr. Pendelton was a friend of the African. His heart was big with sympathy for them and their cause. He had tried all he knew to get justice for them, and, in many cases, he had succeeded in helping those who were being punished unjustly. He shook hands with the two Africans and told them to sit down. Then he seated himself, noticing their sad looks.

"Well, this is a terrible thing! Of course, you had no idea this . . . uh . . . Jonah, would try to escape?"

They shook their heads. The lawyer spoke, "I don't suppose it makes much difference," he said, "but we understand it was no doings of Jonah. His so-called friends – the *tsotsis* with whom he once consorted – engineered this escape. I spoke with one of the policemen, and he reluctantly admitted that Jonah was terrified, and did not want to go. He was practically dragged out of the police van."

Mr. Pendelton shook his head. "Oh, I believe that. By what I

* Council

saw of the young man he did not seem like the desperate, reckless type that, unfortunately, is all too prevalent in our city today." He sighed. "But the fact remains that the lad has broken custody and, as such, he is the object of an intensive search." He leaned forward. "And naturally all those who have tried to help him are suspect." He pointed to the telephone. "You'd be surprised at the vicious calls I've had over that thing. I wish I could have it taken out, but I receive just as many appeals for help over it, so it stays. But the language of those who hate the 'Kaffirs' as they call you – they loath anyone who tries to help you! Still, that's part of my work as a minister of the gospel so I don't complain. I'm simply stating the difficulties of the case." He shook his head.

Gideon spoke up. "Mfundisi, we really value your help. You have given it so freely and helped many of our people. But if they get Jonah back, are you saying that you cannot continue to help in his case?"

Mr. Pendelton sat silently, his face thoughtful. "It could be," he said at last, "that they will just detain Jonah under the new act, whereby – as you know – they can keep a person indefinitely . . . up to ninety days at a time . . . without a trial. The poor lad could languish in jail until he's a middle-aged man – like poor Kaunda and Sosestu and others we might mention. But have some tea!"

As if on cue, a native girl, dressed neatly in black with a white apron, came in with a tray. She smiled at the two Africans, but said nothing, setting down the tray carefully on the table. Then she went out just as quietly. "My wife has trained her well, not so?" Gideon's face was happy. He had secured the maid for the Pendeltons from his church in Orlando, when the minister lost his previous maid who left to get married.

The three sat, sipping their tea and nibbling biscuits, all busy with their thoughts. After a while the lawyer set down his cup and drew a note out of his pocket. "I did not think I should show this to you, sir," he said, "but I guess it is best it should come out." He passed the writing to the rector.

Mr. Pendelton's eyes opened widely as he read. "Who is this from?" he asked.

"A girl. A girl named Miriam. She came to my office. I was out but she wrote these words down and left the note with my clerk." He looked expectantly into the face of the white minister.

"So that's it! It wasn't the *tsotsis* altogether who planned the escape. This – this – schemer Kwanda was in it! It's blackmail! He knew that poor Jonah would be completely in his hands. The lad would do just what he demanded of him because of Jonah's predicament! This puts a new light on it!"

He stopped, resting his head on his hand, and his two native friends knew he was thinking. "I shall go to Mr. Groenewald, the magistrate, and tell him of this. Oh, don't be afraid, I won't say where I got the information. I know we must be very careful not to give Miriam away. Kwanda would kill her. But I'll see that Groenewald gets a clear picture of the situation!"

Gideon still looked grave. "But is it not too late to do anything now, Mfundisi? Surely, by this time, the Assegai, as he is called, has spirited the youth out of the country? It is twenty-four hours since Jonah escaped. Would Kwanda not know that the police would scour every house and shack within miles of the city, and that he would get into serious trouble if he harbored the man?"

Pendelton's face reflected the seriousness of the other two. He nodded. "I did not mean that we could do much to help the boy while he is – or was – in the city. I am just glad we can tell the magistrate and the court officials what we feel is the motive behind the escape. But I have an idea———" His face lit up. "I am booked for an engagement in Salisbury, Rhodesia for Easter. I've been asked to conduct the anniversary services of the Trinity Church there. While I'm there I'll make discreet inquiries about the boy. I doubt if he'll get that far by then – that's only ten days' time. He'll have to travel a good way on foot. I feel sorry for him; how he'll suffer! Rhodesia's the nearest border, so he's bound to go there first. Of course he'll not stay there long – Southern Rhodesia is, as you know, a White Man's country, and they have every sympathy with the aims of this government. He'll make for either Zambia or Kenya. Let's hope I can get to him in time." He paused. "Yes . . . there's something else I can do in the meantime. I'll write to Reverend Sam Webster up there and ask him to keep a lookout. He's got many friends among the natives. In fact, he runs a native church in the Location and it may be he will have heard something about the fugitive."

All three faces had lost something of their cloud as the *indaba* broke up, but before the two visitors left Pendelton, all three men got on their knees and offered a simple prayer for the missing youth—the Accursed One, as Jonah felt himself to be – wandering perhaps in the animal-infested jungle, hopeless and despairing. "May he realize that his friends are praying for him," the Reverend Pendelton closed, and the other two echoed "Amen!"

As the two Africans walked through the streets of Pendelton's parish they were oblivious of the contempt in the faces of some of the White Persons they passed. The memory of the hearty handclasp of their rector friend had put a warm glow in their hearts and verified their purpose in coming.

6

THE RESTLESS, NIGHTMARISH SLEEP of the young fugitive did not restore him at all. Jonah felt worse when he awoke, still in the dark. But the car had stopped now and Tarzan was hanging over the front seat shaking him. "Come, Hyena! We are here."

Jonah sat up and arched his aching back, wondering briefly if the station wagon seat was in fact any more comfortable than the old bumpy car seat he had ridden on earlier. He looked around. The car was parked at the side of the road with the lights out. Although it was still quite dark Jonah recognized the "signs"in the sky. It would soon be dawn. As if to confirm his observation, he could already hear the sleepy twittering of a bird.

"This is it!" Tarzan spoke louder than was necessary. Baswana muttered, half-asleep, half-awake, and cursed the "General" for his lack of consideration. Tarzan laughed and slapped his companion on the shoulder before turning back to Jonah. He threw a knapsack into the back seat. "Here's food for a day, at least. A bottle of beer in there, too. Now, get out. We don't have much time before it will be light."

Jonah pushed open the door and stepped out. He was stiff and cold. His head whirled and he staggered a little. The car was well hidden by overhanging branches and Jonah had to duck to get through them. Baswana remained in the car, "in case of trouble," Tarzan said.

The "General" grabbed Jonah's coat lapels and hissed, "You be noisy and – boom, a bullet in your head, eh? These border guards shoot on sight. Not a sound! Now . . . you got everything – knapsack, coat, money?" Jonah nodded. "Then follow me," ordered the "General."

They walked in the ditch, crouching low. No need to struggle with the bush until they had to. Jonah soon saw the girders of a great bridge looming up ahead. "The Beit Bridge," muttered Tarzan. "Border posts at each side. The guards also patrol up and down the river – the Limpopo – with guns at the ready!" Jonah shivered. Oh, to be back in his home *kraal,* blows, curses and all. At last the "General" turned into the bush. The trees were more plentiful now where the river watered their roots. They stepped carefully, stopping and holding their breath every now and then. Jonah saw the gleam of water ahead, through the trees. Tarzan held up a warning finger.

"We will wait until sentry go by, then we sneak past, right?" Jonah nodded. His teeth were chattering and he wished he were well out of it. The "General" grabbed him again and shook him. "Pull yourself together, *mompara!"* * he growled. "You want to spoil the whole thing?" Jonah tried hard to be calm.

"Sh!" Tarzan pulled him down. Two figures walked slowly to the left, the little bit of light shining on their rifles. "Now! Crawl!" The two black youths snaked through the bushes. "Stay here till I call – like this." Tarzan gave a good imitation of a night owl. "Then come quietly!"

He disappeared, looking for the place where the canoe had been hidden. Soon the bird call came softly. Jonah swallowed hard, crawled quickly through the scrub and slithered down the bank. Under a thick bush he saw a frail dugout. Would he have to entrust his life to that flimsy thing with the river full of crocodiles and hippo? Once more Tarzan had to give him the shock treatment, warning him of the result if he failed.

"Wait here until you see the men go back again, then – when they come back and pass toward the bridge, get going! Paddle without splashing, see? But stay out of sight and get across before they come back. Then watch out for the guards on the other side. They're just as anxious to keep you out as these are to keep you in!"

What a mixed-up world! Years ago, the African had been able to go freely up and down his land, thought Jonah. *Now, we cannot move without a dozen passes, and each country is hemmed in by a border, guarded with guns!* He sighed. How had he gotten mixed up with this business? Even the prison cell was preferable to this. At least he wouldn't risk a bullet in the back there. Should he yell

* Monkey, fool

and let them know he was not in favor of this escape? He shook his head in the dark. It would only bring a hail of bullets. Shoot first and find out what the trouble was after; that was today's motto.

Tarzan was fumbling in his coat pocket. He pulled out a leather folder. "Here! Boss tell me to give this to you – passes. Your new name is Joseph Panzani! Don't forget and blab to everyone that you're Jonah Umlungu! Got that?" Jonah put the wallet carefully into his inside pocket. He must keep that at all cost. His moving about the country depended on those little pieces of paper.

"Soon as I see them go past, I'm off!" Once again his face came close to that of Jonah's. "You mess this up and – you're finished! Understand, Hyena?" Jonah nodded vigorously. He knew he had no other choice.

"Shhh-h! Here they come!" The two sentries walked by again, murmuring in conversation. Tarzan glided away without another word. "Here goes!" said Jonah, despairingly. He got carefully into the little boat, untied the small rope, picked up the paddle, and pushed off. "Better steer right a bit, I think," he murmured. "Border guards not so likely to be down there." He kept his shoulders low, expecting any minute to hear a shout and the whine of a bullet past his ears. But no sound came except the faint splash of his paddle. Suddenly a mighty bulk heaved out of the water ahead of him and he jerked so hard he almost upset the canoe. It was a hippo! Its great cavern of a mouth opened as though it would swallow Jonah, canoe and all. Then it was gone. Jonah's breath was like escaping steam. Then he was across! What a relief! "Thank God!" he exclaimed half-aloud. He still had to make sure the men guarding the Rhodesian side of the bridge did not see him.

He kept under cover as he crouched or crawled for a good mile. By this time the sun was over the horizon and it was getting warmer. Soon the heat would be unbearable – here it was many miles nearer what the White Man calls the Equator. Jonah was glad to lie down and rest. He munched a bit of dry bread and sipped the flat beer, put the food back into his knapsack, and lay back. It was quiet here. There wasn't a sound except the distant hum of a car on the highway. Somehow Jonah felt better than he had before. A fugitive, true; adrift in a strange land, yet a sense of peace filled his heart. If I could only stay here forever . . . away from the troubles of life . . . away from evil men and their mad schemes for power and money. Part of a hymn he had heard at "Hosanna" came to him as his mind sank into slumber:

"Where the wicked cease from troubling
And the weary are at rest . . . ."

Jonah slept, this time peacefully. The African sun rose but it did not bother him under the shadow of a wild fig tree. Suddenly he woke in agony. It seemed as though a thousand thorns were sticking into him. He jumped to his feet like a man possessed of an evil spirit and began slapping his legs, arms, neck and back. "Ants!" Snatching up his knapsack, he ran like a demon through the stunted trees and bushes, beating at different parts of his body and banging the knapsack against the bushes. He was shaking like a leaf. He had lain, without knowing it, in the path taken by swarming "fire ants." He saw the column, a foot wide, like a trickle of molasses moving slugglishly through the bushes. Jonah shouted at the ants as though his shouts would help, still banging at an insect here and there that would not leave him.

His whole body was burning. Oh, for a cooling stream that he could plunge into to relieve the poison of those bites! He saw a gleam through the thorn bushes and pushed his way through. Only a stagnant pool, but better than nothing. He stripped and waded in, the mud oozing up around his ankles. He splashed the water over his smarting limbs and torso. That was better. He took his time and the pain eased somewhat when he brushed mud on the bites. The sun soon dried his body. Jonah pulled on the clothes and shoes Mr. Mukalo had given him and went on. The stinging bites were swelling now, but the mud had eased the fiery pain a bit – there was nothing else he could do. "I will just have to put up with it and hope the pain will grow less. Perhaps if I take my mind away from the thought of it . . . ."

Jonah's mind wandered in a summary of events of the day and what was ahead.

Time to look for a ride. He pushed through the bushes until he heard the hum of an occasional car on the highway. What would happen? Was it wise to hitch a ride? Would he be recognized as a trespasser? He'd have to make up a story. What should he say? "I'm a herd boy. My cattle strayed and I am lost." Ah, the shoes would not do! He took them off and packed them in his knapsack with the rest of the bread. What about the shirt? Too white? He took it off and made it dirtier. No herd boy in the wild bush would have a shirt as clean, although the last two days had not improved its appearance.

Must have a stick! He looked around and selected a straight branch, broke it off and discolored the white end in the earth. All herd boys carried sticks. He would do now.

So Jonah continued his march along the side of the highway, waiting for the right kind of vehicle to come along. He would avoid shiny, new cars. They would be driven by White Men. And a lonely native would be too suspicious. Better wait for a truck, with a black driver. Every time he heard the sound of a motor he looked around, and hid in the bushes if he saw it was not the one he wanted.

It was noon before Jonah heard the rumble of a huge transport truck and saw two black faces in the front seat. He stepped out from the tall grass beside the road and held up his hand. The truck drew up with several spitting coughs as the air brakes gripped. Jonah was greeted with shouts from the grinning Africans. They quickly made room for the youth, and he gratefully squeezed in.

"Sakabona, friend. Where you going? I am Demas, this man Stephen." *Demas and Stephen,* thought Jonah, remembering that Africans always take Bible names. *Our native names usually have something to do with our birth – like "hail" if we were born in a hailstorm; or "measles" if this ailment was common at that time. So we throw them away and take a Bible name. This is good!* After all, was not his African name given as a Curse – *Hyena?*

Jonah was then aware that he had not introduced himself and that the two were waiting to hear his name. He did not think it wrong to deceive the men. The youth thought it wise not to be called "Jonah" or "Umlungu." They might have seen his name in the papers. "I am Joseph," he said. He had always like the story of the lad who had been sold into slavery by his brothers, though a good man, who did not lose his goodness in a heathen land and who rose up to become a Big Baas in Egypt. "I am Joseph!" He told his story about his cattle, and the two truck men did not seem to query it. They were a happy pair, and their loud laughter rang out into the still air. Jonah felt his heart grow lighter. *Oh, that I could be happy like these men,* he thought. *But they do not have the Curse hovering over them like a black cloud.*

"You want to go all the way to Bulawayo or Salisbury with us?" asked Stephen as the great monster started out, with noisy effort.

Should he? Jonah pondered. He felt it best not to go right into the city. He must keep out of sight until he knew what he would do. "Please let me off about a mile this side of Bulawayo – where my village is," he added.

"Okay, Tiger!" laughed Stephen, proud of his knowledge of

American slang. "We stop for a meal a few miles on. There is a place where this monster must get a long drink of petrol."

Demas explained with a grin, "We Africans cannot get away from our old beliefs. One of them is that all moving things are made alive by a spirit. The great locomotive, shooting showers of sparks out of its mouth, is a dragon. The car, spluttering and coughing, sometimes shaking like one with the fever, is possessed of an angry devil. So Stephen was not joking when he spoke of giving this 'monster' a long drink. You want to eat with us?"

Jonah was glad he had the money to do so. He must be careful not to show his big envelope. *If Demas and Stephen saw it, might not temptation come into their hearts?* he asked himself.

So when the truck drew up at a service station he slipped away to draw the envelope out quietly and take out a one pound note in Rhodesian money. He went to the rear of the building, as though he were looking for a rest room, but when he felt in his coat pocket his heart nearly stopped. The envelope was not there! He felt in his other pockets and quickly searched his knapsack. His passes and identification papers were there but the money was truly gone. His heart was like a lump of lead now, but still pounding. He stopped and thought. He heard his name being called – "Joseph, come and eat!" – but he did not answer. Where could it be? He ran to the truck and looked in on the floor. Perhaps he had dropped it when getting in or out of the vehicle. No . . . . He thought hard. *Ah, when I jumped and flailed around after the ants attacked me! Or maybe when I took my clothes off at the pond!* He could picture the white envelope lying on the ground, under the shade of the wild fig tree. There it would lie until the sun and rain rotted it, for no one ever came to that desolate spot. Could he go back? He would never find it; one spot in the jungle or veld was much like another. The Curse again! His mind filled with bitterness and despair. He stood there, a great wave of sadness swamping him from head to foot.

Stephen came out of the cafe. "Come on, Joseph! We cannot stay here long. You must eat quickly!"

Jonah shook his head. The man went inside. In a minute he was out again. "Ah, you have no money, no? Come on in. This we will buy for you, friend!"

Jonah tried to protest. "I . . . I had some money, but I . . . I think I lost it in the woods," he managed.

The African laughed his big laugh. He put his huge arm around the shoulders of the youth. "Come on in!" he said. "You look as though you could do with a good dish of *sadsa!"* Jonah allowed himself to follow. Stephen led the way to the right, where a large sign said, "Non-European." Another sign at the left said, "Europeans Only." He sat on a stool up to the counter and the black man behind it asked Jonah what he wanted. He pointed to the plates of his friends, and the man roughly pushed a big dish of *sadsa,* the "mealie-meal" porridge, toward him. Jonah felt at first he could not eat. His calamity was too hard to bear. But after the first mouthful he realized how empty he was and he ate with appetite.

Demas grinned, "It is good, eh? We Africans do not ask for fancy foods – hot dogs or fried steak. Not as long as we have our *sadsa* . . . good and thick, so thick that, when it is cold it is like a piece of soft rubber. Ah . . . then we are satisfied! That, and a meat stew once in awhile," he added. The others agreed.

Suddenly Jonah felt the eyes of the counter man upon him. He looked up and saw that the man, while polishing a dish, was looking at him with a frown. Jonah went on with his food but was nervously conscious of the stare again. *This man has recognized me!* The Johannesburg papers would have arrived at this wayside station, perhaps that very morning!

Much trouble had made Jonah cunning, like the meer cat that runs across the veld and knows how to dodge the wild dog. He got up and thanked his friends for their kindness. "I will wait outside."

"All right, Joseph. We won't be long," said Demas. Jonah said nothing, but he went out the door. Looking back through the window he saw the scowling counter man go to the telephone. Jonah could see him looking in his direction; then, when he got his party, his lips moved fast and he pointed to where Jonah stood outside the window.

Jonah moved away quietly until he knew that the man could not see him. Then he broke into a run, straight for the bush. No use to continue to ride with Demas and Stephen. The man had spied him! He had phoned through to the custom post. Soon someone on a motorcycle or in a car in a khaki uniform would show up, overtake the truck, and he would be hauled back.

No! I must escape! And his legs moved faster beneath him, his breath coming in hard, dry gasps . . . his knapsack clattering against him as he ran away from the road stop.

7

JONAH FELL IN AN EXHAUSTED HEAP beneath a scrub of bush. The youth sprawled on his back while the earth turned in a dizzy whirl above him. His side ached with the cramp caused by running too fast and too hard so soon after eating. His breath was coming in gulps that he had to fight to get, and his lungs burned from the frantic flight. He slowly rose to prop himself on one elbow as soon as the earth stopped spinning.

Jonah wiped the heavy rivulets of sweat from his face and neck and surveyed the situation. *I feel as though I have run the length of all Rhodesia,* he thought. But it had only been about two miles.

The fugitive began to take mental inventory. The results were far from encouraging. He had lost his money and he had lost his ride. And, he could not hitch another ride now. It was known now that he was on the Johannesburg-Salisbury highway. The road would soon be swarming with White Police. There was nothing to do now but walk. The idea was most uncomfortable. He had thought to ask his new friends the distance to Bulwayo – they estimated about fifty miles. And they knew the mileage well, having driven the run hundreds of times.

He sighed, then did a very strange thing. He rose to his knees in the shadow of the acacia tree where he rested and prayed. Surely the Nkulunkulu did not want him to perish in this wilderness. *I will pray to the Great-Great for help,* he reasoned. *I face evil everywhere. The Curse? Will God, the Great Nkulunkulu, be able to turn the Curse into a blessing, even as the Mfundisi said? Surely He will help me, even as He had come to my aid in sending friends along when I was in prison facing a charge of murder.* He did not know many prayer words, but he had learned a prayer at the mission school. Now he repeated it: "Our Father, which art in Heaven; hallowed be Thy name; Thy Kingdom come . . . ." The part that said, "Give us this day our daily bread" seemed to be the only part that fit his case, and He had already provided that – sending along Stephen and Demas. "Lead us not into temptation" did not seem right, for what temptations could there be way out in the bush? He did not know if the prayer was effective, still, he felt better when he got to his feet. The lump of lead seemed to have lightened a bit. He plodded on, glad for the shoes which he had put back on his feet.

It was now – as the White Man says – something like three o'clock, the sun was still high. Jonah kept well back from the highway. He must put as much distance as he could between the service station and himself before the police came along. They would be sure to search the woods each side of the track. He hurried on, keeping the sun at his left hand and facing steadily north-west. The highway itself was a good guide. He could see the telegraph poles above the tops of the short trees. When he heard the sirens of the police he got farther from the highway. If he could only stave them off until it grew dark he stood a good chance of losing them. He was thankful they were so kind as to warn him of their coming!

On he went, leaping over fallen logs, skirting boulders, pushing his way through thick bushes, some of which tore his clothes with their sharp "wacht-a-bietjie" thorns. Many times he caught a glimpse of a brilliant ribbon winding through the stones or grass. But he was already cautious – had he not seen many snakes in Zululand? The dreaded mamba was the worst, for one died within minutes when its poison coursed through the veins. Lizards darted across his path. His name-sake, a hyena, its hideous laugh startling him, slunk behind Jonah, and he yelled a curse at it. No wonder people hated him – or his name. He loathed the sight of the cowardly beast, with its quick, slinking trot and its evil face; cowardly, too, not killing its own prey, but waiting until the lordly lion downs a deer, then slinking up and snatching bites.

Lions! He started as he suddenly realized he was in lion country. There may be only the odd one in Zululand (although leopards are still common there) but Rhodesia was home to the King of beasts. Jonah prayed again the part of the Lord's Prayer he had skimmed over before. Now it seemed most fitting – "Deliver us from evil."

I must get to shelter before nightfall. Most of the meat-eaters are out after dark. That was also when the mamba and the night adder slithered over the ground, searching for sleepy birds or small animals. He prayed harder.

The sun was hot and his flight was making him sweat heavily. *But I must go on!* He looked around. Nothing but small trees and bushes for miles. He was raging with thirst and was thankful for the small bottle of liquid in his knapsack. He moistened his lips with it and wiped his wet forehead. Then on, quickly, for the night would come all too soon. Then again Jonah heard the sirens, far off to the left. They were on his trail. Nothing for him to do but to run, and trust that he would be invisible among the scanty trees. It was a nightmare of running as he ran and ran and ran, looking around now and then to see if his enemies had taken to the bush in pursuit.

He veered far to the right, as well as north, in his flight. Anything to get away from those maddening sirens. But the White Police must have realized the hopelessness of finding a man in the maze of bushes and trees, for they did not come anywhere near where Jonah panted and ran and hid.

He began to head back toward the road, more to get his bearings than anything else. The sirens had ceased. He could see the tops of the telegraph poles again. On he went, keeping the sun well to his left.

He was now more like one of the White Man's machines that you see in the big fairs, moving not by its own will, but by the White Man's magic. Jonah seemed to hear a voice in his head saying, over and over and over: "On! You must go on! On, on, on!" His heart was racing, pounding against the wall of his chest. Breath came in gasps and his legs moved like the pistons on the monster locomotives. He hardly saw the things around him. If a snake crossed his path, he leaped over it without knowing what he was doing; if a rock or a log got in the way, he would steer around it like one walking in his sleep. His mind was filled with one big concern – to get to Bulawayo.

So he ran with hardly a pause for breath, a sip of beer or a munch of bread until the sun sank lower in the sky. The nature of the scenery had changed. Now he had come to a land where great clumps of rock seemed to start out of the ground for no reason at all. Huge masses of rock, like the castles of the White Man. Jonah could still see the distant highway – or at least the poles marking its path – but all around were these mighty granite pillars. He stopped and looked in amazement. He had not seen anything like this in his own Zululand.

Then he saw the huts, and his heart gave a big jump of relief. Where there were huts there would be shelter, food and safety from wild beasts. Best of all, he knew that these people – living like his ancestors did, away from all the White Man's hard streets, stone buildings and noisy monsters rushing about – would not know anything about the papers and the way they have of telling everything about men who run away from the White Police, or about riots and murders. But he must be careful. How would they receive a stranger? They would wonder where he had sprung from. In their wild state they might attack him. He stood for a long minute – wondering and afraid.

Night was fast coming. He could not spend the darkness in the jungle. He had only two paths to choose from – one led to a night of danger, the other to, perhaps, all that he needed to fit him for tomorrow's journey. The choice was easy as well as quick. He would go to the *kraal*.

He wondered at the shape of the huts. His own people built theirs quite round, like beehives. These were round but the walls were built of mud and the roof was thatched with long grass, like the Zulus', but was pointed like a tent. As he drew near, moving quietly, he saw a group of Africans seated in a circle. In the middle of it a figure leaped and twirled. Even at this distance there was no mistaking this man of evil. He stopped. Should he go on? Would he never get away from the Witch Doctor's black magic? He knew so well what was going on. The chief had sent for the Man-Who-Knows-All-The-Answers. What was it that was causing the crops to wilt, the rains to cease, the cattle to droop, the sickness to come? What the reason was for this Medicine Man's visit, he could not guess. But it held no good for anyone. Was it the same here as at home? Would the Wizard go into a trance and then, under the spell of the powerful spirits, see who was causing all the trouble? It must be someone, and he would point the guilty one out so they could sacrifice him and appease the demons. Jonah trembled as he stood there, concealed by a big rock. Should he venture into such company when he was the Accursed One – singled out by the devils as an easy mark for their mischief? *Better to keep out of sight until this "Smelling Out" was over.* Jonah reasoned.

He crept into a crevice between the huge rocks – a place where he would be hidden for awhile. He sat down, his head bowed on his hands. What was life but trouble? One experience after another, all bad. He felt that his sky was dark indeed, but then remembered there were gleams of light. He must not forget his kind friends in Goldie – the old chaplain . . . the lawyer, Moses . . . Mr. Pendelton – not to mention Mr. Beckwith, who was probably planning to visit the Rand. Or perhaps he had been told not to come because the man he wanted to help had fled. And, of course, Miriam!

After awhile Jonah looked out from his hiding place. Were they finished? No, still in the midst of their *indaba*, the Wizard, with his white-painted face and noisy dangling charms was prancing around like the wounded wildebeeste.

It was dark now; Jonah looked up between his rocky shelter and saw the stars so far away, so mysterious, so powerless to help. Somehow the words of the prison Mfundisi, spoken low in the cell, surged back into his mind when he thought of the pagan rites going on a few hundred feet away:

"Where He displays His healing power
Death and the curse are known no more . . ."

Jonah knew by what he had seen of this tribe that the healing power of the Great-Great had not been displayed. No missionary had visited this remote place; or, if he had, his words were as the straw in the rushing waters, swept away in a moment to be heard no more. A daring thought came into Jonah's mind. Should he try to tell these fellow Africans of what he had learned from Gideon? Suppose he ran out now and called out "Stop! All this is wrong; it is bad! This man is leading you down the path to death! It is not devils who have brought your sickness, your failures, your blights——"

He sighed at the hopelessness of the thought. How could he, the Accursed, dare even to hope for one moment that he could do any good? Did he have anything to give them? Out of his little stock, did he have any gift for these ignorant, dark heathen? If he had only owned a small Book – like the one the Mfundisi had read to him from in the cell – he could have "made the Book talk." He had long since lost the little Gospel of Luke he once owned. Living among the *tsotsis* had not helped him do much reading, especially books like that.

Jonah took a careful look and dodged back quickly. He saw the Witch Doctor coming toward him! He prayed that he had not been seen, but he need not have feared. The Wizard was mumbling to himself as he passed and a bad smile wrinkled his painted face. Jonah knew why he seemed pleased. He was driving before him two fat goats and a sheep. Under his arm he held a chicken, its legs tied so that it should not escape. It squawked in anger. It looked as though the Medicine Man had been well paid for his work.

Jonah waited for a comfortable while, then walked–fearful, uncertain – toward the encampment. The Africans were now clustered around a fire, over which a huge iron pot swung from a chain on a tripod. A smell that made Jonah hungry was blown to his nostrils by the breeze as he came nearer. Suddenly the chatter of voices ceased. Jonah went hot and cold as all eyes swung round and focused on him as he walked slowly toward the blaze. He stood there wishing he had the powers of the Wizard and could have whisked himself a hundred miles away – he felt so fearful. At last an older man, a big muscular warrior, struggled to his feet, came forward, and said, "Who are you?"

No need to hide his real name any more. "I am Jonah," he said. "I was lost in the jungle. I would like to stay the night. Tomorrow I go to Bulawayo."

Jonah noticed a strange look come into the man's eyes. One moment he had looked rather cross at this stranger coming uninvited to his feast; the next moment his eyes lit up with what seemed to Jonah to be an almost sinister look and he held out his hand. "Welcome; I am Chief Senekulu. Come and eat, my son," he said. His voice sounded friendly but Jonah could not forget that look. The others made room for him and soon he was seated on the ground around the campfire, a gourd full of hot stew was before him, with a big home-made wooden spoon. Questions came thick and fast as he ladled in the welcome food. It was the first *good* meal he'd had since he had left the prison. He was glad of the excuse of eating his food to cover up any delays in his answers, but he thought he had satisfied their curiosity.

They spoke Zulu, though with a curious accent that Jonah found puzzling at first. It was a long time ago that their ancestors had trekked to this part of Africa, driven out by Chaka and his bloodthirsty warriors, and the language was bound to change. *What a blessing I can understand them,* he thought. *I do not know what I would have done if they had spoken a strange tongue.* Still, he had mingled with many tribesmen from different parts of Africa – all who had come to Goldie to seek their fortune – and had picked up a few words of Swahili, Shangaan, Nyasa and other queer tongues.

Jonah's heart felt a warm glow as he listened to the carefree chatter of the Matabele natives. His mind went back to Zululand, to the few occasions when his Curse was forgotten and he could mix with the young people of the tribe and, for awhile, feel he was like the others – not a marked man because of the Curse. There had been times among the *tsotsis* when he had almost forgotten that he was an evil-wished one, but it had been brought back to him with much force by the shooting. But here, among these Africans who knew little about the big city, he felt at home.

At last the hungriest one among them was full. He gave a satisfied belch and the eating came to an end. The big pot was taken away and logs thrown on the fire. "Must keep fire going," said a young warrior who had sat next to Jonah. "Lions and leopards like to visit us!" Jonah liked him. He was full of laughter and had seemed happy to refill Jonah's dish more than once. His name was Pondula. The chief struggled to his feet, saying as he did so, "You must stay the night – and as long as you want. See that *kya?*" He pointed to a hut on the fringe of the group of dwellings. "You can sleep there; it is empty. Kuloopi went away to the White Man's city and has not yet come back."

Jonah thanked him. He stayed with the young people who were preparing for an evening's enjoyment. Pondula and others had assembled to sing, and soon the pulsating rhythm of African music punctuated the cool, still night air. Again Jonah was taken back to Zululand. The "Russians" – the Goldie gang – liked to imitate the American rock-and-roll singing. But here it was like home. Anyone who wanted to or felt like making up something that was real, something that was happening, would raise his voice and the rest would join in the refrain as kind of an answer to the question sung by the singer.

Jonah liked it. There was much laughter as Pondula sang about one Kadumo who, so the song said, that day had been bending over to pick up a stick of wood when Bopo, the goat, had butted him, so that his head went into a gourd of sour milk that had been "ripening" in the sun.

"How he chased the goat,"

sang the chorus,

"But Bopo knew how to dodge a fat man . . ."

Many verses were sung and Jonah marveled at the clever way Pondula made up line after line. Other songs followed; then an older youth with a scarred and unhappy face struck up a line. It seemed to Jonah that a chill fell over the group.

"An evil person has put a spell on our kraal . . ."

although they all chimed in, rather feebly:

"The witch doctor knows who it is, and he will die . . ."

The gloomy one went on:

"This night the curse shall be broken . . .
The wrong avenged.
And our kraal will know the warmth of the sun . . ."

and again the refrain:

"The witch doctor knows who it is, and he will die . . ."

Jonah shivered. He felt the youth with the unhappy face had

looked at him very strangely as he sang. And the chorus, seeing the singer doing that, had also stared at the stranger.

Jonah turned to Pondula. "The days of 'smelling-out' are over, not so? Surely the White Man will punish any return to the tribal laws if it takes in killing?"

Pondula whispered back, "Our chief is not afraid of the White Man's laws. He has done some bad things in his time and has not been caught."

Jonah did not like to show fear or suspicion, but why had they stared at him so? Now it came back to him. He had seen the chief stop and say something in the man's ear as he left the feast. He thought he could trust Pondula. "Why do they stare at me? I have done no wrong to the tribe!"

Pondula looked around fearfully. His face was no more filled with laughter. "I did not see them stare at you, my friend," he answered low. "Besides, a stranger should have no fear. He should be protected from all harm. Do not fear. The chief has shown you where you are to sleep. Go and rest from your weary journeying. I shall see that no harm comes to you!" He pressed Jonah's arm and Jonah felt glad that he had at least one friend here.

"I think I shall go now," he answered. "I have traveled far and am tired." Silence fell on the group as he stood up and said, "Good night, my friends, and thank you for the food. It was good!"

They replied with a chorus of "Good nights" as he walked toward his hut. Jonah found it, like his own *kya* at home, bare, save for a calabash or two hanging from the thatched ceiling by strings and a ring of hard mud in the center for a fire. The floor was of dried mud, too, but Jonah was used to that. There was a wooden "pillow," like a little stool. He needed a blanket – it could get cool in the night – so he crawled to the low opening that served as a door and looked out. Pondula turned his head, and seeing Jonah, jumped up and came over. "Have you a blanket, my friend? No? I get one." He returned quickly with a blanket. Jonah thanked him and gladly wrapped it around him, put the "pillow" under his head and fell asleep.

He always dreamed more when he had eaten before going to bed. This night Jonah saw many strange things in his sleep. Great fiery monsters, out of whose mouths came sparks and an awful sound – like the police sirens, only much louder. He tried to run but they pursued him, through trees and over streams – nothing would stop them. Then, as he ran – slowly, with heavy limbs – a man whose face was painted with white rings rose up from the ground, his open mouth full of lion's fangs. Jonah was caught between the White Man's monsters and the Witch Doctor; his legs would not move; he was doomed ———"

Jonah came back to reality with a jolt. Someone was shaking his shoulder. "Wake up, my friend!" It was Pondula, whispering in a voice that was edged with urgency. "Wake up! You were right!"

Jonah sat up, his mind still spinning from the nightmare and this sudden arousing. "What – what do you want?" His voice was stammering.

Pondula stooped and whispered in Jonah's ear. "I remembered what you said about Sekatuni – the man who sang the song – and I went quietly to his hut. His wife said he was not there; he was visiting the chief. I crept behind the chief's hut and heard them talking."

Jonah's heart became as lead again. He knew what was coming. The Curse was as potent as ever – even in this remote spot. He reached out and caught up his knapsack, his only possession, and began to strap it around his shoulders. He knew he would have to leave his shelter and go on – on and ever on. When would this aimless pilgrimage cease? Only when he died?

Pondula was speaking – whispering excitedly. "I remember now the Witch Doctor did say that it was not one of us that had caused the blight of sickness. And it was not the Munyumbwe, the tribe in the next valley. It was, he said, a stranger, who would visit our *kraal within the next going down of the sun!* Then *you* came into sight!"

"But–but do you not believe the Witch Doctor, as the others do?" asked Jonah, in spite of his fear.

Pondula's face broke into one of his happy smiles – there was just enough light to see it. "I went to the mission school," he said proudly. "My father is also a chief. And old Senekulu, our chief, knows that. It's too late to explain it now – it's a long story. I am not under Senekulu's fist like the others. But you must go! I heard them talking. They said that, at dawn, you are to be taken to the top of the highest rock and hurled down – just as Chaka used to hurl his victims – first getting his executioner to crush their skull with a frightful blow from a knobkerry war club! It is called the Rock of Execution. Below is a deep pool formed by the river. There lurk the crocodiles———"

Jonah's scalp felt as though an ice cold scorpion were creeping on it. To think that savagery lurked in the backveld as though the old, bad days were back. Not so frequently perhaps, because of the danger of the White Police finding out. But in remote places who knows what evil practices go on? Who is to tell if someone is missing? With many wives, babies are born every day and the tribe grows. What census taker can keep track of the many thousands of Africans?

"Here, put this in your bag," said Pondula. He handed Jonah some strips of sun-dried meat, called *biltong* – hard as wood, and looking like sticks. It was nourishing, easy-to-carry food that would not spoil. Jonah took it gratefully and stowed it in his knapsack. "They will not come until the sun has finished his sleep and comes back to earth. You can rest more if you like."

Jonah shook his head. "Thank you, my friend. I have had some sleep. I feel rested, and the food strengthened me. I think I will go. How far must I walk to reach Bulawayo?"

"The highway is about a mile that way," Pondula whispered and pointed. "You may catch a ride to the city. But watch out for lions. There is a family of them in a patch of jungle by the river. Come, I will show you the way to go!"

Jonah and Pondula crept through the low doorway, Pondula going first and reporting that no one was in sight. Jonah followed and both stood to their feet. It was a fine night. Jonah looked up at the stars, twinkling so serenely far overhead. How could they look down so calmly when such great evil dwelt on the earth? How could the place, bathed in moonlight, seem so like a paradise when wickedness lived in men's hearts? He sighed. In a way, he did not want to leave this place. He had found a small spell of happiness – the friendship of his own race, music, talk, laughter and food. Now he must turn his back on it and face the unfriendly world.

"There," said Pondula, pointing. "Keep that bright star in your gaze and go on. The big city is about a day's journey. I hope you reach it safely and find your own people again."

Jonah faced his friend. He gripped his hand and thanked him for his kindness. "You have saved my life. Perhaps some day I can do you good!"

Pondula's strong, white teeth gleamed in the starlight but he shook his head. "Some day I hope to go to the city and learn to be a doctor," he said. "But, as you may have seen by the White Man's papers, there is much trouble in our land. In the meantime I stay here, away from it all. Goodbye! *Slala gahsli!* Go safely!" Another handshake and he turned and glided away among the huts. Jonah hoped fervently that Pondula would not find trouble for his part in helping him escape.

8

JONAH HAD NO IDEA what time of the night it was. He guessed around midnight. The moon was high in the heavens and the stars were bright.

He stepped out as bravely as he could with brisk, long steps putting distance between himself and the *kraal* very quickly. It was true. The Curse had worked against him again. Yet, he did not feel as frightened. In fact, a sense of peace was strangely present in the young fugitive's heart. *And,* he reasoned, *if the Curse is all-powerful, how is it that my life was spared?* Something was happening. The power of the spell was weakening! Could it be that the prayer of the prison Mfundisi had reached the ear of the Great-Great, somewhere out there in that vast universe? Were the prayers of his other friends in Goldie checking the power of the evil demons that made sport of him all his life? Jonah would try to believe that it was so.

His mind had been very active and the night air invigorating. He had stepped off nearly a mile of space between himself and those at the *kraal* who would sacrifice him if he stayed.

Should he make for the highway now? He thought not. There would be few cars and trucks at night. Perhaps it would be better, though not any safer, to press on through the veld and jungle while it was dark. Then when he did make for the road, he would be that much farther from the point where he had left the truck when he thought the man had phoned the police. The sound of the sirens that same afternoon made him realize he was probably right.

Jonah walked as silently as he could. He had decided not to put his shoes on – he was used to walking in his bare feet and it made less noise. He did not want to attract those animals that seek their meat under cover of darkness. Jonah was tense, every nerve alert, looking to the right and left, now and then swinging around to see if the slinky hyena was creeping up on him in the dark. He saw nothing. He also kept a watchful eye on the ground and avoided patches of long grass. The last thing he wanted now was a leg poisoned by the swift-striking mamba.

Jonah kept as far away as he could from the patch of jungle Pondula had warned him of – where a family of lions lived. He was making good progress! He must not only get on to his destination but also put as much mileage as he could between him and Old Senekulu's *kraal.* Suddenly a tremendous roar came from behind a clump of rock. Jonah froze beside another rock. As he crouched, he prayed and hoped. The first roar was followed by a whole series of roars. Jonah's throat was dry – he swallowed hard.

Then it happened. A kudu bull, magnificent in its graceful, sturdy form, with curving horns, bounded just in front of him. His shadow was followed by a flash of tawny lightning. A lioness, her fangs reflecting the moonlight, her face a mask of savage fury, sprang from the bush. Jonah was paralyzed but he had sense enough to realize that it was a good thing. One move and the killer might have been diverted from its prey. Then he saw a sight that he would never have believed if it had been told him. The great animal suddenly turned and lowered its head. Unable to stop her flying leap, the lioness landed full on the bayonet-like horns! Screaming in pain, she managed to pull her wounded flank off the antlers, to make a second attack on the kudu. The animal, head still down, was pawing the ground in front of the lioness. As the female retreated slightly the bull turned and bounded away, disappearing like a phantom into the shadows. The bleeding beast lay growling and licking her wounds. A haughty male lion sauntered out from the rock. Jonah's heart thudded more. The young lions joined the group and the three stood looking without concern at the female.

Jonah knew his own position was dangerous. The lions would not exert themselves to chase a fleet, aggressive foe. But if they knew a defenseless young man hid nearby, his life was worth little. So Jonah knelt, shivering and praying that the slight breeze would not carry his scent to them. At last the female decided she had tended her wounds long enough; she limped away, the lions stalking after her.

Jonah waited until he was sure they were well away, guided by the moans of the lioness and hungry growls of the others as they grew fainter and fainter. He was more alert than ever now. Anything could happen in this wilderness. He skirted trees that were taller than he – although there were few in that part – for who knew whether a leopard might be crouched along a limb, ready to pounce on the careless traveler!

It was a nerve-racking night. Many times Jonah started as a scurry in the bushes told him something was around. One time he clambered into the limbs of a tree just in time to escape an angry wart-hog, and wasted a half hour while it grunted and rooted at the foot of the trunk. Finally it shuffled away when a jackal trotted by, and Jonah climbed down, stiff and sore.

At last the stars paled, the moon disappeared, and the sleepy chirping of birds became a welcome sound to the weary wanderer's ears. Jonah began to veer to the left. He must get a lift. He was utterly weary from the hard trudging after his short sleep. He kept his eyes open for a sight of the telegraph poles. At last! He sighed audibly in relief. In a few minutes he was walking along the paved road, looking back now and then for the sight of a vehicle. The first to come along was a private car – one that shone in the early sunlight like a toy. That wouldn't do. He flopped unceremoniously into the ditch as it sped by. The next and the next he let pass him. Then, with a welcome rumble and roar, a lumbering lorry chugged into view. When he came nearer Jonah saw a good, old black face under a shapeless hat. His own people! How his heart warmed at the sight.

The driver slowed up when he saw Jonah's hand wave. There was a sign on the windshield that said "No Riders," but the driver swung the door open and Jonah clambered up. He sank into the seat, glad for the rough feed sack that served as a cushion. "Other man, he sleep in the back," laughed the African, another happy specimen of the Bantu. "Me Goliath!"

"I am Joseph!" Jonah thought it best to take his false name in case the truck drivers had been warned about the fugitive. "I go Bulawayo and Salisbury!"

"Me too!" laughed Goliath. "Say . . . you not, by any chance, man police want, eh?" and he laughed heartily at his joke. Jonah's heart almost stopped. So his case was so well known! No doubt all truck drivers had been notified to watch out for the fugitive.

"I . . . I . . . come from Senekulu's *kraal,*" he stammered.

The driver laughed. "I just joking! I hear they catch that man in Salisbury!"

"Caught him?" Jonah was very attentive.

"Yah. At least they catch one man police want much!"

Jonah breathed with relief. If they had caught someone whose plight was like his own perhaps it would take the pressure off his pursuit.

The driver was an amiable man who believed in whiling away the long hours by singing. His deep bass voice rolled out into the still morning air as the truck roared along. Jonah's head nodded; soon he was fast asleep. The movement of the vehicle was like the motion of a mother carrying her *piccannin* on her back – snug and cosy in its blanket – and Jonah slept as soundly as if he were on the floor in his own *kya.*

"Hey, move over!" It was another voice that aroused him. A grinning face peered through the canvas that hung down back of the seat, between the seat and the interior of the truck. The assistant had awakened. "Who are you?" he asked. Jonah grinned back. He gave the same reply he had given to Goliath. "Me Timothy!" said the man as he climbed over the back of the seat and squeezed in between Jonah and Goliath. Goliath pulled over to the side of the road, stopped the vehicle and disappeared into the truck.

"I feel like a good sleep now," he said, and Timothy took his place at the wheel. On they went, the big van eating up the miles, though noisily. Jonah dozed again. Timothy did not sing like his partner – he wanted to talk, and Jonah found it hard to stay awake long enough to listen to him.

Something the man said suddenly stung him awake. "The guards at the river getting very fussy," he grumbled. "An African got 'cross the river in a dugout, or some kind of boat, and they found it on the Rhodesian side." He laughed. "Poor chap lost his money. The guards found a packet of banknotes lying in the boat!"

So that's where I lost it, thought Jonah. *Not in the bush!*

Timothy went on. "Police soon find out where money came from. Lots fingerprints on envelope. Soon catch man who cross border. But I hope he get away!"

Fear fought with hope in Jonah's heart. The White Police could find a criminal by the lines on his fingers. Kwanda's fingerprints would be on that envelope! He knew his were, but what did that matter? His were already filed away in the White Man's iron boxes. Perhaps this would lead the police to the Big Baas – Kwanda. *If only he were arrested and put out of the way, I would not be afraid,* said Jonah to himself. He knew now where he wanted to go in Bulawayo.

"Where is the native Location?" he asked Timothy.

"On this side town. You go there? Plenty good restaurants and beer-halls. And a place to stay for us natives! You can bet it is as far away from the White Man's homes as can get! They no like to smell us!" He laughed uproariously.

Jonah knew that if he got any help or information it would be from the Africans – his own people – not from the Whites. Besides, there was nowhere he could stay in the white section. "Non-Whites Stay Away" signs were everywhere.

Now more and more *kyas* and little shacks appeared at the sides of the road. Once in awhile a proper brick house, with real drapes at the windows, showed that some natives had prospered and climbed out of the pit of poverty. After a few more minutes they ran through a White Man's suburb – grand homes, with cars in the driveways and trees all around. A bus full of singing shouting Africans passed them, and Timothy shouted a greeting. Natives clad in shirt and shorts flashed to and fro on bicycles and motorcycles. All seemed laughing and happy in spite of the unrest supposed to exist in this White-dominated land.

Timothy slowed down and pulled over to the side of the road. He pointed across the huddle of tin-roofed shacks. "There the Location! Good luck!" Goliath stuck his sleepy face out of the canvas.

"You go now, Joseph? *Slala gahsli!"*

Jonah shook hands and jumped down. "Thank you, Goliath and Timothy! The ride was good. You have helped me!"

Timothy put the truck in gear with a roar, blasted his horn – sending a crowd of Africans laughing and scuttling out of the way, and the truck rolled on. Jonah stood there a moment looking after it. Another link severed. Would he find as good friends in the Location as he had on the highway? Where could he go? He had no money; no friends; no prospects. Not until he got to Zambia and saw "the Lion," Simba.

Well, he could work. Surely a willing native could find a job to tide him over until he could get transportation to Zambia. He began to walk toward the recreational part of the Location. He was already in the native quarter – shacks were all around him, their occupants busy cooking their midday meal. It was strange to watch them trying to make city life as much like the home *kraal* as they could, using tripods and iron pots in the back or front yards. There was plenty of noise and movement and Jonah felt strangely excited. It somehow reminded him of the native districts in Goldie, yet it was different. Some of the shouted words he understood – it was of the speech of the Matabele, cousins to his own Zulus. But some was like the chattering of the baboons – what the White Man calls "gibberish."

Jonah had many different feelings that were jumping inside him like the hopping of the frog. He was glad to be here, away from the White Man, with his own people. Yet at the same time, he was apprehensive about what would happen. He would have to spend some time in finding an answer to the puzzle. But he was sure one would come to him.

A long low building with dirty white-washed walls and a corrugated iron roof seemed to be the place of activity. Jonah was both tired and hungry as he walked toward it. He was jostled by men coming out as he pushed his way through the door into the crowded hall. A long counter stretched from end to end, with several tables taking up the floor space. The room – a combined cafe and saloon – was dark and blue with the haze of tobacco smoke and loud with jovial boisterousness of drinking and eating Africans. Although he knew before searching, Jonah felt in all his pockets. Nothing. He looked hungrily at the sandwiches and other eats on display behind the counter.

A slap on his back staggered him. He turned around and was confronted with the laughing face of Demas, the burly driver of the first truck.

"Hi, Joseph! Where you spring from?"

Jonah looked wildly around for a way of escape, but there was none. He was hemmed in on all sides by carefree men who did not know or even notice him.

"Don't be afraid, *muntu!* Do you think I would turn you in?" The big voice was softer and his laugh stopped the fluttering of Jonah's heart. Demas must have talked to the man behind the counter who phoned the police.

"What – what happened . . . after I ran away?" His words came jerkily. He was still afraid Demas might hand him over to his enemies.

"That bad, cross man? Ha!" Demas made a sound like the wart-dog through his nose and for embellishment added several words of cursing. "I told him what I think of him – telling the border guards on one of our own. I know you not guilty of murder! Not so, Stephen?" His partner came up, taking huge bites out of a Danish pastry and sucking a bottle of American cola through a straw.

He swallowed before speaking. "Aw, we know you are not a

murderer. What is that they say – you were 'framed.' Yeah . . . that's it, you were framed. Yes?" They all laughed together.

The rest of the crowd was oblivious to the reunion. "Come and sit down, Joseph. You have had a hard time and are hungry, yes? Have a meat pie . . . or some stew!"

Jonah was grinning widely although his eyes were ready to unleash a flood of tears. Expecting to be turned over to the authorities one minute, the next, invited to eat. Delivered once again. *It is true! The Curse is not so powerful now.*

"You . . . you know that I cannot pay———"

"Yes, yes. We know. But are not friends for such times?" asked Demas. Stephen nodded his willingness to help the youth without taking the straw from his mouth.

"I . . . I thank you both so much. It is too much to expect———"

Again the black truck driver interrupted. "Save your mouth for the eating of food, we will talk later."

Demas selected a table, told the other two to sit, and went to the counter. He came back with hot food that made Jonah's nose twitch and his mouth water. "Now, tell us where you go, what you do. We want to help you, no?" said Stephen, who was now finished with his food.

Jonah did not reply. His mouth was full, and he satisfied his hunger while the other two looked on with big grins. At last he laid down his knife and fork and looked his friends in the eye.

"I thank you for your kindness," he said. "I will tell you all about myself. But we cannot talk here. Will not others hear?"

"Why not in the truck?" asked Demas. "We're on our way again. Will you come with us?"

Would he! This was what the Mfundisi called "guidance" – that he should have reached this spot just at the time his two friends were there; that they should be going on to Salisbury – surely the Great-Great had planned it!

Stephen went to the counter, paid the girl what they owed, and the three walked to the truck. It was parked near the spot where Jonah had left Goliath and Timothy. Seated in the front, in between his two friends, Jonah told them his whole story.

"Kwanda bad man," grunted Demas. "I hear of him many times. He say he working for Black Man; I think he working for the Reds!" Stephen agreed.

"Do you think I should go back?" asked Jonah.

"Well, we could take you when we get through at Salisbury,"

said Demas doubtfully, "but you would be picked up at once. The White Man does not like to be made a fool of. You have jumped out of his trap – oh, I know it was not your doings – but they do not care about that. Your sentence would be much more – much worse."

The truck roared along the road. Demas did not want to go through Bulawayo for he knew the traffic was heavy and he wished to go on to Salisbury where he would unload his goods. So Jonah never saw Bulawayo – the "Place of Killing" the city had been named for.

"Your only hope," said Stephen, "is to prove your innocence. If you could find out who shot the man–you say your leader Tarzan? Perhaps it was he; perhaps one of the others. How you find out?"

Jonah's face was cloudy. "They would never tell on one another," he said. "Tarzan would kill anyone who betrayed one of the gang."

They rode on in silence. Their thoughts were busy with the big problem – how to find the real killer so that Jonah could be set free. Suddenly Jonah had a thought. "Tarzan was the only one who had a gun," he said. "He said it made him the real leader. He would not let the others have a gun; only knives."

"Then Tarzan is the killer," grunted Demas.

"Yes, but it would take more than Mr. Mapomulo – is that the lawyer's name – to prove it," added Stephen.

There was a heavy pause while the three thought.

"I tell you what I do." Stephen spoke out in a loud voice after the truck had traveled a good while. "When I get to Goldie I go to see Mr. Mapomulo. I tell him what you think about Tarzan and the gun. He is clever enough to find out the truth. Okay, Tiger?"

Jonah grinned. Would it do? He wondered if it were the best thing. It would let his friends know where he was, although by the time Moses got on the job he might be many miles away. Still, it would do no harm. "I thank you if you do that," he said to Stephen.

It was a long journey. Jonah spent it sleeping, eating at wayside cafes and talking over his problems. His heart was much lighter. Things did not look so hopeless. The thought that he would have to be a wanderer from nation to nation – never to see his home again (or Miriam) might not be a true picture. He had not thought of finding out the real murderer before his two friends thought of it. *If I could only be free again!* His heart lifted at the prospect. Free to make up for the mistakes and follies of the past – especially his sojourn in Goldie. He would link up with the church, with Gideon's congregation, and he would go to school. Yes, and he would get a good job and, perhaps, (his dreams were rosy) marry Miriam. Then his heart sank again. It was only a dream. The Curse was still hanging over him – like an evil vulture, waiting to swoop down. The truck rolled on monotonously.

9

VILLAGE AFTER VILLAGE and town after town were passed. Then the usual signs of a big city showed up – more huts, more shacks, more houses. Finally from a ridge, Jonah found himself looking down on a city of tall, white buildings – like Goldie, only not so widespread. Salisbury looked clean-cut and sparkling white in the light of the full moon. But Jonah knew that all was not as it seemed. There was something sinister in those neatly-laid-out rows of perfectly-shaped, graceful, tall flats and offices. Stephen and Demas had told him a lot about Rhodesia and this, its capital city.

"They say the African must be well-educated to be able to vote," Demas had told him. "Four years high school. But where are the schools? Oh, yes, plenty primary schools. You know how many were able to vote last year – that is, men who earn £300* a year and go to high school for four years? Only about 200! Why? Because there not enough high schools for us Blacks!" He spat in his disgust.

"Still, the same rule applies to Whites," put in Stephen, who was not so excitable as his partner. "Those who cannot qualify for 'A' voters' roll go on 'B' roll – and there are both Blacks and Whites on this roll!"

Demas only grunted. Nothing would convince him that the Whites were fair to his people.

"And what about this 'independence' I read of in the Johannesburg papers?" asked Jonah.

Demas was driving now so Stephen could use both his hands in replying. "You see, this country was still under rule of Britain, right? Britain want every Black Man to have vote, right away. But this

* About $900

Big Baas, Ian Smith, he says no. Much trouble if Africans get vote; sweep all Whites out of country. Wouldn't that be good?" He laughed gleefully.

"So Mr. Smith broke away from England?"

"That's right! We Africans wanted England to send her soldiers and airmen and make the Whites surrender. But Wilson, Big Baas in England, say no. We make 'em give in by not sending them any more oil or petrol for their cars. That soon bring them to knees."

"And has it?"

Stephen and Demas both looked somber. "Not yet! Why?" said Demas, excitedly. "Because South Africa gives her lots petrol, that why!"

"That's what we've got in the back of truck," said Stephen, with an ironic smile. "Men like Kwanda and other union leaders in South Africa make trouble for us. We get beat up one night. See this?" He pulled open his shirt collar and showed a nasty scar, partly healed. "We feel sorry for our brothers here, but we must think of our jobs – and our lives!"

"Well, it not come all from South Africa," said Demas. "Some come by ships through ports on coast – Beira and Dar es Salaam. *Hard* to keep the White Man from getting his petrol."

Now the truck was rolling along paved streets. Jonah saw that not many persons were out. "Is what they call 'curfew' – it sounds every night so natives have to be to bed," grinned Demas. "White people stay in for fear of trouble."

White Police, in khaki uniforms, strolled about in twos. Police cars with red lights blinking from the top cruised the streets. One stopped as they were driving up a street; a man jumped out and lifted his hand. Demas put on the brakes and fumbled in his pocket for a card when the truck stopped. The policeman poked his flashlight into the cab looking at each face carefully before taking the card, shining his light on it to read.

There was a long pause while the man checked the permit. Jonah held his breath.

"Okay, drive over to the government warehouse. Know where it is, I suppose?" They nodded. The man waved them on.

"Not much chance of trouble breaking out. They've put all the Black leaders in prison," grumbled Demas. "But you can't sit on a snake's hole forever. It'll bite you and make you get off!" His laugh was not so happy this time. The fate of their Rhodesian brothers was heavy on the hearts of these two Bantus.

"You go back tonight?" asked Jonah.

"No, we sleep at the Location. You stay with us and we take you there after we get rid of our load."

The petrol and oil depot was surrounded by high barbed-wire fences, with flares and searchlights lighting up the grounds. Many big sheds had been put up to take care of the oil drums and the petrol tanks. Other trucks were unloading their goods with metallic clanging sounds. Guards stood around, their bayonets gleaming in the light of the flares. "Be a great bonfire if Simba could get his men to set fire to this," said Demas, under his breath.

"What chance of getting in!" Stephen was more realistic. A sentry waved them on and another man showed them where to unload. Some Blacks had been willing to do this work – work which meant beating the embargo of the English. Sweating Negroes, stripped to the waist, men of big muscles, handled the drums like so many gourds and the truck was soon empty.

Jonah had kept in the background – he did not want to answer any questions. It was a wonder that he had not been queried when the policeman stopped them on the street. Jonah guessed that the country was too tense over the embargo, and too anxious to see that supplies of oil and other necessary things got through without bothering about an escaped criminal. So he was left alone and much relieved.

"All aboard!" sang out Stephen. Away they went, his two friends happy now that their work was done. "We take back a load of tobacco tomorrow," continued Stephen. "That is one thing that might break them down. How can they sell all those millions of tons of tobacco? Our country cannot take it all!"

"England used to take most of it?"

"Yes! Great smokers, the English!" They laughed.

The Location was much like the one in Bulawayo. Demas arranged for Jonah to have a room and a good meal. "You're on your own tomorrow," said Stephen. "What will you do?"

"Get a job!"

"Why you no apply at government warehouse? They need lots of strong men."

What a laugh, thought Jonah. He, who was supposed to be going about recruiting men and money for the liberation of his own country, was willing to "work with the enemy" as it were! Well, it would only be for a short while. He only wanted just enough money to tide him over. It was not good to have to take gifts from others, with no chance of paying them back.

He slept well that night. The bed was rickety and the mattress very thin, but after lying on the ground it was luxurious. The sunlight streaming in at the small window woke him. His first thought was for Stephen and Demas. He slipped on his clothes, went out and ran across to the beer-hall, but they were not there. Then he remembered that truck drivers must make an early start. They had already gone. Jonah felt an empty feeling near his heart. He had grown fond of these two hearty Africans. Now he was entirely alone, without a friend in a strange, new city – surrounded by unknown dangers.

He was hungry. *What should I do – look for work feeling empty?* No. His encounters had given Jonah nerve, if not complete courage. He went up to the buxom girl at the counter. "You remember me? I was with the two truck drivers yesterday."

The girl nodded and showed her white teeth in a smile.

"I have no money. But I get work today. Okay if I pay when I get my money?"

The girl hesitated for a moment, then with another laugh she agreed. "I keep close tab on you, my friend," she said, as she made a note on a pad. "What do you want now? Porridge? Tea? Coffee?"

Jonah felt that the sun had broken out again from behind the clouds. He was learning that facing life with courage – not letting the Curse have its way – was better than moping like a sick cow. Courage and, of course, prayer. He knew the good friends in Goldie were praying for him, and he was beginning to feel that life was not altogether dismal. He had a good meal, cleaned himself up with a shower and shave. He washed out his shirt and put it out in the hot sun to dry. Then he made his plans for the day. He would seek work at the only place he knew – the government petrol storage center. Failing that, he would try somewhere else, and keep trying until he found something.

Someone had placed a Bible in his room and Jonah opened it. It was in his own tongue and an encouraging warmth came over him as his eyes fell on the words he had read many times at "Hosanna." The Sermon on the Mount – the words of the great Ujesu Kristo: ". . . Blessed are ye when men shall revile you and say all manner of evil against you falsely for My sake. Rejoice and be exceeding glad, for so persecuted they the prophets that were before you . . ."

The glow in his heart spread throughout his whole body. This was he – Jonah, the Hyena, Umlungu! Men were saying all manner of evil against him. The papers were full of stories of "this desperate *tsotsi,* who had not only slain a White Man, but had actually broken away from custody!" Anyone reading the papers would curse him as a wicked, reckless Kaffir – typical of the lawless element that infested the slums and shack-towns of the Rand. He knew the White People were saying, "We ought to *do* something about this menace. These niggers have gone too far. It's about time we shot a few of them!" The White Man expected the Kaffir to live in a little shed at the back of his garden; to work for starvation wages; to live on a little mealie-meal and meat! As for the mine owners, they kept all their workers – 350,000 of them – in compounds, as prisoners. They were not allowed to leave without a special pass. True, they fed them well, but paid them only one twentieth of what the White workers got. Then they became stirred up when Black Men rebel at their injustice.

Jonah forgot all the injustice he was going through. Someone knew all about it – the Great-Great understood. Oh, Jonah knew he was not entirely innocent. He should not have run with the *tsotsis;* he should have gone to the Mfundisi's church; he should have remembered what Baas Beckwith had told him. It was all his own fault for choosing bad company. But he was not as bad as the papers said he was. Nor was he as bad as what the White People were thinking of him as they turned on their radios to hear about the escape of "this unprincipled scoundrel, roving the country, a menace to all whom he meets." He put the Bible down and looked out the window. Everything seemed beautiful, even the dreary unbaked brick shacks, with their rusty roofs and scant shrubbery, trying so hard to grow out of the baked red soil.

Jonah went out and retrieved his shirt. He felt cleaner than he had been for days. He shined his shoes, brushed his coat and pants, and felt he was ready to face life again. He pulled out his wallet (*what a blessing I didn't lose that, too,* he reminded himself) and looked at his passes and identification. He saw that he was one Joseph Panzani and that he was supposed to have worked in a number of places with strange names. "Small, out-of-the-way places, I think," murmured Jonah, "Kwanda must know Rhodesia well to fake passes like this! I hope no one asks me questions about these places!"

Jonah found Salisbury to be a beautiful city, with well laid out streets, lined with trees, paved roads, sidewalks, stores as big as those in Goldie, tall office buildings and many cars. It seemed the gasoline embargo had not stopped traffic very much. Signs of prosperity were everywhere, but the people looked tense. The Africans looked angry. There was a nervous haste in the walk and look of the White People. Their eyes had a faraway look in them, as though they were wondering what the future would be. Jonah passed a travel bureau and saw it filled with Whites. As he went on a man and woman came out studying long tickets they held in their hands. Jonah heard the man say, "Ship sails on the 29th. Can't be too soon for me!"

It seemed to Jonah that some people were leaving Rhodesia, afraid of the "blood bath" that the papers had predicted would come. He tried to think of the place less than a century ago – when it was bush, just like what he had recently come through. Demas had told him there were less than half a million natives then, living like his own Zulus off grain grown by scratching the soil with a home-made hoe. Now the natives were healthy and prosperous – four million of them. The White Man had brought big machines – things with big teeth that really broke up the earth. One farm alone could grow 10,000 bags of mealies or Indian corn. True, Demas had said, the Africans did not get much money for working for the White Man, but they were not starving.

Perhaps it was a bit unfair of the Africans to demand independence – the right to rule their own country. They would be taking over a much different nation than the one they had given to Cecil Rhodes – a bit of western civilization, with great ranches, dams, bridges, a network of highways. But were the Whites really doing what England insisted on – training the Africans to take over? Why had they not started fifty years before when the country was young? Did they not deliberately keep the Black Man as a "hewer of wood and a drawer of water?" What was it his people called it? Jonah reached back into his brain for the answer, long forgotten. Yes – "White Supremacy."

Jonah did not know exactly what the words "White Supremacy" meant, but he could see the principle at work. He could not see the White Man working side by side with the Black, on the same footing. All the Whites he had seen – except perhaps for the good Mfundisi – had only spoken to him (or other natives) to give an order, never to ask them how they felt or "What time is it?" or "Could you tell me the way to the railway station?" No, Kaffirs were only fit to order about; not intelligent enough to converse with.

Jonah's thoughts were sadly mixed up as he walked through the streets of this lovely town; with its lovely white bungalows, its bougainvillea, hibiscus, jacaranda and flame trees. Contrasting was the sight of its well-dressed anxious Whites.

It was a good walk from the Location to the place where the government had stored the contraband gas and where they doled it out strictly, but Jonah was glad for the exercise and diversion. The sun shone warmly and the air was not too humid.

"Go to that office over there," said the sweating native to whom Jonah spoke when he had passed the sentries at the big gates. His heart was beating a little faster than usual as he knocked on the door and waited, for an African must not walk in like a White Man does. He must be respectful. If he wears a hat, he should hold it in his hand. If he smokes, he must throw the cigarette away. Nothing arouses the anger of a White Man more than to see a Kaffir who "does not keep his place." Jonah had seen men thrown out bodily from places where the White Man was the lord – for not being obedient enough, or forgetting to "keep their place." So he walked in quietly and stood humbly, waiting for the two Europeans to look up from what they were doing and notice him.

He might just as well have been invisible. The two began to talk. It was about the races that were being held the next day. "I put thirty bob on 'Swinger,' " said one, lighting a cigarette. "Got a tip!"

The other leaned back in his chair, and put his feet on the table. "Don't stand a chance! I put my money on 'Atom Bomb.' Now there's a winner, if you like."

Jonah waited patiently. Suddenly the first speaker strolled over to the counter and stubbed his cigarette into a tray. "Well, what do you want?"

"Sebenzi, baas! Work, please," said Jonah, placing his wallet, open, on the counter.

The man picked it up and scanned it skeptically. "Hope you're not one o' these agitators," he said. "We don't want any of them around here!"

Jonah shook his head emphatically.

The man looked at him rather closely. "You don't look much like the natives around here," he said. "Got a different cut to your jib, if I may say so! Where do you come from?"

Jonah turned hot and cold. He was glad he could not blush, like the White Man, with his fair skin. He stammered something and pointed to his pass.

"H'mm . . . a country chap, I suppose. Well, are you strong? Gotta have muscles for handling these oil drums. We can only offer you night work. Midnight to eight. Okay? I'll write you out a pass. You'll never get past the guards without it."

Jonah nodded eagerly. "Start tonight then. Thirty bob a week. Don't be late! Here, let me take your name." He scribbled something in a book, said "Okay" again, and Jonah knew he was dismissed. His head whirled as he stepped outside the office, but he was elated. He had stood the test. The man had not asked any questions about his past; he had accepted his new name without any bad looks. Best of all, Jonah had a job and would be able to pay his way – at least to earn enough so he would be independent until he got through to Zambia and – his mood changed quickly – met Simba, "the Lion."

But Jonah felt good as he walked away from the petrol depot. Oh, if he could only shake off the past and really be free to work, to save money, to woo, to wed–Miriam's face flashed into his mind–and to be happy. Happy? He? – the Accursed one? A fugitive? A man under orders from the evil Nathaniel Kwanda? But the sense of joy trying to bubble up from somewhere deep within him would not depart. "Blessed are ye . . . ." Not cursed; blessed. If only he could believe that! That those words meant him.

Jonah stopped in amazement. He had come to a big stone building, set back in lawns and gardens. But what surprised Jonah was the sight of the Africans there. They were wearing nice clothes and carrying books under their arms, walking about these grounds. And, wonder of wonders, White Men walked among them and did not trouble to keep away from the Blacks! Then Jonah read the words on a big board at the gates of this place: University of Rhodesia. He had never seen such a big school before! There may have been one in Goldie but he had never seen it. Here was a school where Africans were able to live on the same footing as White Men! *Maybe this Rhodesia is better than my own land after all!* Yet the liberated nations around were dying to crush this land. They were shouting to the English to send planes and guns to destroy the White Man here.

Jonah walked on, shaking his head. This was too much for him to understand, so he reviewed it all. First, he knew he hated Mr. Kwanda. He had forced him to do something he did not want to do – stir up trouble for the Whites, to get the warlike Africans of other nations to send spies and agitators to his own land to make bloodshed and strife. Jonah did not like it. But what could he do? *I am like the twig that falls into the stream, swept along against my will. I am helpless!* thought the fugitive

But again he did not believe it with his whole brain and heart. Again that feeling would bubble up – that he was not helpless so long as the Nkulunkulu was there–somewhere in the nearby shadows. He had heard the song at the mission, "keeping watch over His own." Hopeless as things seemed, Jonah felt something would happen to save him.

Jonah had left the rich part of the city. He was getting near to the Location where the difference was almost dramatic. No quiet gardens; instead, lots of children running about; tin cans and rubbish instead of green lawns and bushes. *These things cost money,* thought Jonah. *My people cannot afford to be clean and tidy.*

He noticed a man peering out from between buildings. His hands were full of papers. Jonah thought the man looked carefully about him and seemed somewhat afraid. He saw Jonah coming and motioned for him to come into the lane. Jonah stopped. Should he do what the man wanted? He went forward a step or two and the man thrust a paper into his hand. It was headed "Zapu" and was covered with a writing that did not make sense to Jonah.

"What's this?" he said, in Zulu. The man snatched the paper away and gave Jonah another – this in his own tongue. The man was whispering and still looking about in a fearful way.

"You come to meeting, no? Room back of beer hall. Three o'clock."

"What's it all about?"

"You come; you see!" And the man was gone, back into the shadows of the alley.

Jonah knew that a meeting of more than two or three Africans was not right in the eyes of the White Man's law. That is why this man was so frightened in delivering his pamphlets.

Jonah walked toward his room, reading the paper. It seemed that this "Zapu" was the Zimbabwe African People's Union. Demas had told him that the Africans hated the name Rhodesia. To them it stood for all that was bad in the White Man – his arrogance; his cunning; his boldness in stealing their land, then labeling it with the name of the man who had stolen it – Rhodes. "No, our land is Zimbabwe! Not Rhodesia!" All this was included in the tract Jonah was reading.

Jonah left the paper in his room and headed for the cafe.

An idea had been forming in Jonah's mind – he would write to Miriam! He went up to the girl at the counter and told her he had a job. She grinned cheerfully. "Good! You pay at the end of the week, no?"

He nodded and asked her to give him a plate of stew and a chunk of bread. Then he asked her for a pen, a stamp, an envelope and a piece of writing paper.

"Here, you take this writing pad. You may spoil one page," she laughed. "I'm keeping track of all these things!"

After he had eaten Jonah went to his room and wrote the letter. How much should he tell Miriam? He knew she worked in his great enemy's office, but he also felt she had no sympathy with Kwanda's aims. Jonah decided to tell her to pass on to Mr. Kwanda the news that he had lost the money given him and was forced to stay in Salisbury for awhile. So he began:

"Dear Miriam." A warm glow came over him as he scratched the words on the linen paper. It was almost like speaking to her face to face. She would unfold his letter, take this very sheet of paper into her hands and read the words that came from his heart.

"Your dear face has never been out of my thoughts . . . ." he wrote. That was true. To think that he had only seen her for such a short time – yet she had walked right into his heart. In the car journey she had been with him; crossing the river; trudging fearfully through the jungle – her face like a bright star on a dark night.

"Someday when I am able to clear my name of this terrible charge I hope to come back and then . . . ." Jonah hesitated. He dare not say much. He did not know what her thoughts were toward him. Perhaps she already had a lover. The thought stopped his pen for a moment and he stared unseeingly out of the window. Should he bother to write? Would she not laugh at the very idea of this unknown fugitive daring to think of her? He picked up the sheet of paper, ready to tear it in two. Then he knew he would not. *Wonderful things have happened to me since I left prison,* he said to himself. *I am not going to think bad things. I will think of day, not night. Sunshine, not clouds.* He continued the letter, mentioning that he would make his way to Zambia in a little while and see the man Mr. Kwanda had asked him to see. He mentioned the good friends who had helped him on his journey, then signed his name – his real name – and addressed the envelope. "Miriam . . . (he did not even know her last name), c/o *Africa Speaks,* Johannesburg."

That should get to her. Surely that paper was well known. It had caused the White Man many sleepless nights! Then he put the letter into the envelope and stuck on his stamp.

It was getting near three o'clock when he finished. He went out, slipped the letter into the nearest post box and walked to the back door of the beer hall. Other Africans were making their way quietly toward the place, all of them walking as though they were being followed, looking to the right and to the left, then behind them.

There was a smaller hall behind and Jonah followed the crowd through. A man at the door looked at him with eyes that seemed to look into one's heart but he said nothing. Jonah went in and sat near the back. Soon the seats were filled. Jonah looked about him with interest. The men were all Black, dressed like himself in a shirt, pants and coat. Some were in shirt sleeves. None wore ties except the two men seated on the platform. All were talking to one another in low tones. Every now and then they looked around at the door, as though expecting the police to break in and arrest them.

Two other men came in from the back. One was – Jonah could tell by his bearing–a leader of men. He was not tall but his shoulders were broad. The man's eyes, under heavy brows, were shining. He had a short beard, in the custom of Africans, and his walk was quick and sure. A man stood up and pointed to him, saying, "Eli Kamanga, head of the Zapu in this town!"

Kamanga stood quickly and raised his hand to stop the clapping, although it was subdued. "We have no time to waste," he said. Jonah did not understand the words he spoke but the other man repeated them in Zulu for those who did not understand Shona. "As you all know, our White Lords (he smiled a bitter smile) will not let us meet together. They are afraid of words. Why? Because our words cut like spears!" He stood. His face was hard and his eyes like fire. Jonah knew what hate was at that moment – the hate of the African for those who had oppressed them and denied them freedom of speech in their own land.

"We haven't much time. At any moment we might hear those hateful sirens and see the cursed White Police with their guns and clubs. You all know that the White Monsters have defied those who want to help us gain *Uhuru* and are determined to *keep* us down." He looked around, and then his voice came softly, hissingly. "Our friends in Zambia are helping us! Their country – what used to be called Northern Rhodesia – is hurt by this blockade. For one thing, the railway goes through both countries, and these people"–he waved his hand toward the city – "are making it hard for the Zambians to get their copper from the mines."

The Africans were leaning toward their leader, almost holding their breath, their eyes fixed on him. "Sabotage! You know what that is. That is our only weapon now. Later there will be armies moving in to kill! kill! kill!" He worked hard to keep his voice down. Little flecks of foam whitened his jaw. Then he mastered himself. "You all heard of the three men who were brave enough to throw hand grenades into the snackbar on Speke Avenue? That is good! You may injure people who have done us no harm, but that does not matter. The White leaders will soon see that we mean business! Many Whites were hurt in that explosion. Too bad the African waiter was hurt, but we must be ready to sacrifice some to gain the battle." He paused and wiped his wide forehead.

"We are not doing enough, nor are the things we do bad enough to cause much trouble. We must think *big* thoughts. Now, if we could – say – blow up the armories where the White Soldiers have their weapons, that would be good. Or the home of the Prime Minister . . . ." He paused to see what effect his words were having.

"Another great victory would be to set fire to the petrol dump!" Jonah felt as though someone had suddenly put a cold hand on his neck. He hoped his start was not apparent. But no one seemed to notice it. "Does anyone here work there?"

Jonah studied the floor. Men were turning and looking – perhaps not at him, but at anyone who might be at the back who worked with the petrol. It was a bad moment for Jonah. He shifted in his seat but did not raise his hand. The last thing he wanted was to get mixed up in Rhodesia's troubles. And a revelation came to Jonah. He knew at that moment he was not in sympathy with violence. Perhaps his short life among the *tsotsis* had shown him the folly of hatred and strife. It only begat more violence. Surely there must be a better way!

Kamanga was speaking. "Time is on our side! Take the United Nations. Every new country that gains independence, no matter how small, can get a voting voice in the U.N. It has a voice equal to that of the mighty Russia, or the decadent United States, or weak England. Out of 119 nations," – his face now wore a triumphant grin – "there are at least eighty Black or Yellow nations. Think of the power we wield in the world today!" The Africans were stirred by his eloquent words; their eyes shone. They might not all have understood what their leader said about world affairs but they knew the Blacks were coming into their own. They were no longer the underdogs, to be kicked, bullied and kept down.

Jonah looked around carefully. No one was looking at him. He got up quietly and walked out on tiptoe, passing through the beer hall on the way to his own room. Just as he closed the door he heard the siren. Looking out his window he saw White khaki-clad figures running toward the beer hall, with clubs and guns in their hands. They disappeared. In a few minutes they came out again. This time they were struggling with black natives, pushing them toward the big vans with much shouting and swearing. *Thank God I left!* thought Jonah. He did not see Eli Kamanga's sturdy figure among the captives. He had heard the leader always escaped – he was crafty and quick and almost seemed to know ahead when danger threatened. He had been known to slip into a trapdoor in the floor and lay low until danger had passed. Kamanga had probably had some such emergency exit this time, and at the first sound of the siren had acted, leaving his less intelligent followers to fend for themselves.

10

THE REVEREND MICHAEL PENDELTON pushed aside the papers that littered his desk. He turned to his visitor, Moses Mapomulo. He gave the lawyer much work, for he knew Moses was thorough in things of the law. The pastor often wished he were well-versed in legal matters, for many of the members of his African parish were in need of this help. There were so many White Man's laws; it was hard to keep out of trouble. There was the question of passes. It was difficult to keep from losing them. Then there was the constant trouble of moving. The African didn't like moving – having to leave a place, no matter how tumble-down it was, to go to far away new places the government had built for him. If you did not move as quickly as the officials thought you should the White Police would come – without any words – with a truck, and throw your few things into it. They then "persuaded" you (with a gun) to get in beside them, and off you'd go. Mr. Pendelton knew that Moses Mapomulo would find a way out if there was one in all these tangles.

"Heard anything about the fugitive? Young . . . ah . . . wasn't his name Jonah? Last I heard he had been forced by this notorious Kwanda to cross the border and do secret agent work for the rebels."

The lawyer folded up his spectacles and placed them in his pocket. His face brightened. "Strange you should ask that, sir," he replied, his deep voice booming out in the quiet room. "A man called on me the other day – chap named Stephen, a truck driver. Seems he picked up our man, although Jonah is going by another name."

Mr. Pendelton stood up. "Let's go into the other room; it's more comfortable. I've asked Miriam to bring tea – oh, that's my latest new girl," he laughed. "We just have time to train these maids when they up and get married. But this girl is an interesting case. She worked for this Kwanda."

Moses nodded. "Nice girl! I know her. She came to me about Jonah, you remember?" The two moved into the lounge and the minister indicated a chair. The lawyer sat down carefully. It was a chair with much padding, not like the hard ones he had at home. "I see by the papers there was a raid on Kwanda's office. Apparently the police found out he was implicated in this escape."

"Yes, something to do with fingerprints found on a packet of money – foreign currency. Evidently Kwanda gave Jonah money to help him in his undercover work and he lost it in crossing the river. That gave Kwanda away. A good thing he's under arrest. A dangerous man.

"And the *tsotsi* leader, Tarzan, was arrested, I believe."

There was a tinkle of china-ware and a tall girl walked in silently. Moses thought she looked beautiful in her black dress and white apron. Her eyes were bright and she seemed to have something she wanted to say.

"Excuse me, sir. Did I hear you speak of . . . Jonah?" She seemed a little nervous at being so bold as to interrupt her *baas* and his visitor.

Mr. Pendelton looked surprised. "Just set the tea down there, Miriam. Yes, we did not want anyone to hear. It is rather a private matter."

Moses looked at her with his deep-set eyes. Miriam set the tray down gently. She looked embarrassed. She fumbled in the pocket of her apron and pulled out an envelope. "Please excuse me, *Baas,*" she said, her voice shaking. "I–I like this young man . . . feel sorry for him. I was there when they brought him . . . from the prison van." The red showed through the brown of her oval face. "I–I had to take him food when he was locked in the garage – when he was hiding from the police."

"And what is this?"

"It is a letter from Jonah! I got it the very day I left working for Mr. Kwanda."

The two men were on their feet. "May I see it?" asked the cleric.

"Of course! I go now!" Miriam walked quickly from the room.

"I see it is postmarked Salisbury," murmured the lawyer.

"Rather risky, his writing, isn't it? Jonah could be extradited in no time. Seems to me he must be very fond of this girl to risk imprisonment by writing and giving away his whereabouts."

The clergyman handed his visitor a cup of tea and passed him a plate of cookies. "What were you saying about a man who called on you?" He sat down and helped himself to tea, opening Miriam's letter as he did so.

"This chap was a truck driver journeying with a companion from Johannesburg to Bulawayo and Salisbury. They saw a rather forlorn figure on the highway some miles past the border and gave him a lift. Of course he told them an untrue story and they felt a bit suspicious of him. Anyway, they gave him a meal at the first way-side station, but when they went out to resume their journey he had disappeared. Good reason why! A waiter had recognized Jonah from his photo in the papers and had phoned through to the border post. They looked to see if they could pick up the fugitive farther on but no sign of him."

"Poor lad! No doubt he took to the woods?"

"Here's the sequel! When the truck drivers got to Bulawayo, who should they run into in the native restaurant but Jonah! He was frightened when they spoke to him but they assured him they wouldn't turn him in."

"Seems he left Bulawayo and is now in Salisbury."

The lawyer set down his cup and leaned forward. "This man Stephen told me an interesting fact, one that might help us to get Jonah off! He told Stephen what he was accused of and insisted he was innocent. Then he said something he had forgotten before, that only this man who calls himself 'Tarzan' carried a gun! As leader he wouldn't let any of the others use one. He let them have knives or blackjacks but no guns!"

The minister looked thoughtful. "That seems to prove conclusively that this Tarzan is the real murderer! But how to prove it!"

The deep voice was lower, but still resonant. "We've got to find that murder weapon! The police have kept the bullets that killed the merchant. I checked on that and they told me if I could find the gun they were fired from, and prove the ownership, it would do a lot toward clearing Jonah Umlungu!"

The clergyman nodded and went back to his tea. Moses continued. "Do you suppose it could be hidden around the newspaper office? These *tsotsis* had rooms there. It's a kind of a community center, you know. I would guess that when Tarzan knew he was about to be arrested he hid the gun in the first place he could think of. By the way, what is happening to the paper? I wouldn't like to see it closed right down. Under good management it would be an excellent outlet for the Africans."

Mr. Pendelton's face lit up. "I agree! As a matter of fact, I've got a fine young chap in there. A fellow educated at Fort Hare, name of Malesela, John Malesela. You must know him; he's been teaching. I took him to see the Minister of Information and he agreed to the appointment. Mind you, he has to clean up a lot of dirt! Seems the Commies have been supporting the paper – or helping to. But John and his new co-workers are pushing the advertising possibilities. Ads are pouring in. Lots of white merchants are glad to pay for ads in a decent African paper. Before they wouldn't. They didn't like the tone of the paper. But it's going fine now. But getting back to your original statement – about the gun . . . ."

Moses stood in his excitement. "Sir, would you be able to get me in there so I can search for that gun?"

"Certainly! I'll give you a note to John right away! You just may have something."

He opened Miriam's letter again. "Not much in this! Seems a rather tame and nervous love letter. But he does give us one clue. He's planning to go into Zambia and 'see a certain man Mr. Kwanda asked me to see.' I don't like that!"

"Jonah will be getting into dangerous company. I imagine Kwanda put him in touch with the worst rebels in that area. If he makes that connection———"

"I hope I see Jonah when I go up there next week for the Easter services. I've already written Webster about him. No doubt he's keeping his eyes open, or getting some of his Black friends to do so."

Mr. Pendelton called Miriam and she came shyly, with head bent and her hand to her face.

Mr. Pendelton's voice was kind. "You seem to like this . . . this unfortunate youth; and he evidently likes you – enough to risk re-arrest by sending you this letter." He turned to Moses. "I think we can trust this young lady. Please don't say a word of this to anyone. I want you to know that we three – Mr. Gideon Mukalo, this man, Mr. Mapomulo and I – have been interesting others in Jonah's case from the beginning. We think, as you do, that he is innocent. Of course, he made a bad start on the Rand by getting in with these *tsotsis,* but he has learned his lesson, I'm sure. He is taking the blame for a crime one of his bad companions did. Mr. Mapomulo here is trying to prove his innocence."

The friendly Black looked at the girl closely. "You know Kwanda's place pretty well." The girl nodded. "Where did Tarzan stay? Did he have a room of his own? We're trying to find the gun he must have used to kill Lipshotz, the merchant who was shot in the robbery. Now think!"

Miriam did not need to think. She answered at once. "He and this other bad man – Baswana – have same room." She tried to tell her *baas* and the lawyer how to find the room. "You know where the big machine that make the noise?" The minister nodded. Miriam motioned with her right hand. "Just past there – in the corner." She made a face. "I know it well! Always full of beer bottles when I go to clean it each day."

"I think I'll find it all right," replied Moses.

The minister smiled at the girl. "Here's your letter. If Jonah clears his name, we'll get him a good job and I think he'll settle down and do better. It wouldn't be wise for you to write him, but if I see him – I'm going up to Salisbury soon – I'll take a message from you to him. Right?"

The sun shone in Miriam's face. She turned and left the room with a light, quick step.

"All things work together for good to them that love," quoted Mr. Pendelton. "I think there are possibilities in that young man and his prospects are brighter now than they've been for a long time. Quite a lot has come out of this morning's work. Strange that I should have seen Miriam when I took John to his new job. I just offered to take her out of there and let her train as a domestic. Why, she jumped at the chance. My wife has taken to her. Liked her from the start. Ah . . . but time is slipping by. Let's have a word of prayer."

The two knelt and again earnest prayer went up for the wanderer. Thanks were offered for the prospects that had opened up for him and the cleric prayed that he would be divinely protected in the dangerous places to which he might go. "And, Lord, bring peace to this troubled continent – and justice!" finished Mr. Pendelton. Moses uttered a fervent "Amen!"

"Now for the note!" The minister went back to his desk and scribbled a few words on a sheet of note paper. This he placed in an envelope, writing the name of the new editor, John Malesela, on the front. Moses took it gratefully.

"Let me know how you get on," said the pastor, shaking hands. "And if there's anything I can do, let me know that too!"

Moses left with a warm feeling in his heart. If only all the White Men were like him, this would be a wonderful country, he said to himself.

He waited at the corner for a bus. Several came and went, but he did not get on them. He stood there a long time, patiently waiting, for an African must learn patience in the White Man's country; that is, if he will use the White Man's machines. At last he saw the red monster rumbling along toward him. It bore a big sign on the front, "Natives Only." It stopped, the grinning African driver nodding cheerfully. "Morning Baas! Lovely mornin'!"

The vehicle took Moses within a few blocks of the office of *Africa Speaks*. He mounted the stairs and knocked on the office door. He didn't know that this was the door through which Jonah had walked so fearfully to meet Mr. Kwanda. Instead of the fat neck and the shiny bald head, a tall young African man sat behind the desk. He rose to greet his visitor. They knew one another a little.

"Mr. Mapomulo, the lawyer, not so?" Moses nodded, presented his letter, and quickly told the editor of Jonah and his problems.

Mr. Malesela led the way past the press room to a door in the corner. "I'm afraid this place has been the haunt of much evil," he said. "I know we Africans are oppressed, but it is useless to try violence and subversive means to get our country back again. Now, this paper can be a powerful weapon for justice."

"I agree," replied Moses. "If you keep on publishing the truth – in a moderate way – it is bound to make an impression."

"This is the room Tarzan occupied with Baswana. He's gone, too. Got away just before the raid, I understand. I've gotten the rest of the gang to leave. They made a fuss about it but I told them the police would keep their eye on this place from now on. That decided them! Now, if you'll excuse me, I'm trying to get out this week's issue!"

"Certainly! I'll let you know if I find anything!"

The editor went back to his office. Moses pushed open the door of Tarzan's former room and looked around. Mr. Malesela had had the junk cleaned out, and all that remained was a small bed and a cot. (Evidently Tarzan, as the leader, let Baswana have the cot.) These and a washstand completed the furnishings, except for a battered chair. The lawyer went to the most obvious hiding place for a gun – the bed. He lifted the corners of the mattress and felt all around but found nothing. The small drawer in the washstand revealed nothing. He opened the closet door but it was bare of everything except a lonely bent coathanger. He felt all along the high shelf but it, too, was bare of everything – except dust.

"Wonder if he had time to pass the weapon to Baswana before his arrest?" mused the lawyer. "Couldn't have done that! If Baswana could have gotten away Tarzan stood the same chance. No! It's got to be here!"

He even opened the window and looked around to see if, by any chance, he might find a shelf or box nailed outside that could have hidden a gun, but there was nothing but the unpainted woodwork and a rusty hook that at one time had held one end of a clothesline. He closed the window and slowly paced, in deep thought.

As he walked across the floor Moses felt a board squeak under his weight but he was too preoccupied to realize its significance at first. Then he brightened, stooped and examined the floor. A dirty mat lay alongside the bed. He lifted it and saw it covered a short board that looked as though it had been removed more than once. Moses took out a pen knife and pried the board up. His heart gave a jump – there lay the gun! Mr. Mapomulo did not touch it at once. He took out his handkerchief, carefully placed a corner of it around the barrel of the weapon and tossed it on the bed. Then he walked into Mr. Malesela's office and told him of the discovery. "Have you a big envelope I can put it in?" he asked.

John picked up a brown envelope and walked back with the lawyer to Tarzan's former room. "I see you don't want to get your own fingerprints on it! Good idea! To think that a bullet from that gun brought a man's life to an abrupt end!"

"And it may save the life of another!"

Moses carefully picked up the gun with his handkerchief, and while John held the envelope open he slipped the revolver in. Then he sealed it and placed it in his briefcase.

"Thank you for your help, Mr. Malesela! Don't put any of this in the papers yet. When the story breaks I'll be sure you get the 'scoop.' "

"Don't worry!" replied John. "I'll keep it dark until the proper time. And I sincerely hope the court will accept the evidence and prove that Jonah did not kill the man!"

They shook hands and the lawyer ran down the stairs with a feeling of hope, giving his long legs added momentum.

11

THE REVEREND MICHAEL PENDELTON answered a knock at the manse door. His two Negro friends, Gideon Mukalo and Moses Mapomulo, stood there. The lawyer carried a briefcase.

"Come in, come in!" said Mr. Pendelton.

"Are you busy, Mfundisi?" asked the lawyer.

"Of course!" he smiled. "Did you ever know a minister that wasn't? But I'm sure your business won't take long. Come in, my friends. Come in!"

When the three were assembled in the front room, Moses opened his case and drew out the revolver.

"You found it, then?"

"Yes, sir! Thanks to your friend, Mr. Malesela. He gave me free access to Tarzan's former room and, just when I thought I'd drawn a blank, I found it under loose floor boards."

The minister must have watched a few TV dramas, for he took his handkerchief out and picked the gun up gingerly by the barrel. "Ugly weapon," he said, and his face showed his disgust. "We make it too easy for people to get these lethal weapons. Almost anyone can get one and bring sudden death to innocent men." Then he grunted, "Looks like a .32 to me!"

"Yes, the paper said it was a .32 bullet that killed Mr. Lipshotz," said Gideon. "Now, sir, we want to ask you a favor!"

The pastor laughed. "I suppose you want me to accompany

you to the C.I.D.* headquarters? I'd tell you to go by yourselves only I know you'd get scant attention from the police. Sure, I'll go; if I can do anything to bring about justice for Jonah, I'll do it. When did you intend going?"

"Just when it suits you," boomed the lawyer.

"We'd better phone first. These chaps can make it awkward if you don't clear the way. It'll only be a wasted trip if we go when they won't see us."

He went into his office, looked up the number of the C.I.D. and got through to a Sergeant DeVilliers. The man's voice was very cool when he knew who was phoning and his reason for the call. "It's rather unorthodox, sir," he said. "We like to unearth the evidence ourselves. This savors of a 'put-up' job——"

Mr. Pendelton broke in. "What are you implying, sergeant?" His voice was cutting. "A put-up job, indeed! Do you think——?"

"Don't get excited, sir." The sergeant's voice was deliberately insolent. "We've got to watch these Kaffirs. You can't trust them, you know. They'll do anything to get one of their own off the hook!"

The parson was breathing heavily. He managed to control his indignation. "When can I see you about this weapon?" he demanded. "Or must I get through to Colonel DuPlessis?"

"Oh, come right away!" The sergeant's voice was more polite. "We'll hand the gun over to the ballistic experts. It'll take a day or two to get their report back, so you'll have to be patient."

"Right! We'll be right over. You're on Simmonds Square, right?"

Mr. Pendelton returned to the other two. He did not say anything about his talk to the sergeant. "Let's go, my friends," he said.

Moses carefully slipped the revolver back into the briefcase. The minister led the way to his car.

The White Police on duty looked as though they were smelling a bad odor as the trio walked through the main door and passed their desks. It is not "proper" for a White man to walk with a Kaffir!

"Sergeant DeVilliers?" asked Mr. Pendelton.

"Third on the right! Have you got an appointment?"

"Yes!"

The sergeant did not rise but offered the minister a chair. He ignored the two Africans so they all stood. "Now, let's have a look

* Criminal Investigation Department

at this gun." The sergeant lifted it carefully from the case. "How about fingerprints?"

"This man, Lawyer Mapomulo, was very careful when he found the weapon not to blur any that might be on it!" said the pastor.

"H'mm!" The sergeant's voice was very skeptical.

Sergeant DeVilliers slipped the gun into a big envelope. In a business-like tone he said, "Okay . . . you can leave this with me."

Mr. Pendelton looked at him closely. The two Africans were satisfied and were at the point of walking out, but the White Man stayed. He did not trust the C.I.D. officer. "Is that all?" he asked, his voice cool and aloof.

The officer looked at him. His brows drew together. "What do you mean?" His voice was like sandpaper.

"I want a receipt." The minister smiled but his eyes were hard. He had had many dealings with these White Police and he knew that when it came to natives they were inclined to be harsh and tricky.

For a moment the two men stared into one another's eyes. The Afrikaner, sullen, tall and heavy, jaw like a rock. The Englishman shorter, slight. He was a man you could sweep aside with a breath – so it would seem – but something in his cool, steady gaze made the policeman turn his eyes away.

"Oh, all right!" His voice had a growl in it. "You chaps are a jolly nuisance!"

"A little more politeness, please!" The minister's voice had an edge on it, like a saw.

The C.I.D. man snatched up a pad, scribbled something on it, tore a sheet off and handed it to the other. Mr. Pendelton did not place it immediately in his pocket. He examined it carefully. "H'mm! Right date; right name; right description. Yes, I think this'll do, Mr. DeVilliers! I'll expect a report on this weapon within the week." He fixed his eyes again on the glowering sergeant. "If I don't hear by the end of the week, mind you, I'm phoning through to Colonel DuPlessis! Do you understand?"

The sergeant's face grew almost purple. He clamped his lips to stop from blurting certain words. At last he managed a "good-by!" and pointed to the door.

"Come on." Mr. Pendelton walked with a step that did not hasten. It was a step that was firm. The two Africans looked at him in respect. Alone they would have been shouted at, bullied, put off with no redress and no promise of action. That would have been the end of the gun. It would have dropped out of sight, and Jonah's chances would have dwindled to zero. They would have gone back and made respectful inquiries, only to be met with sneers and insults. In time they would have stopped inquiring. They would have been able to go no farther.

By the end of the week Mr. Pendelton had heard no news from the C.I.D. "I'll give DeVilliers one more chance," he told his wife. He picked up the phone and dialed a number. His voice was quiet but cut like a knife. "Put me through to Sergeant DeVilliers," he said.

"Why don't you speak Afrikaans!" snarled the voice at the other end.

"Do as I say or I'll report you!" Mr. Pendelton's voice was as snappy as he ever allowed it to be.

The man growled something in his own tongue and switched through the call.

"This is Reverend Michael Pendelton," said the parson when he heard the familiar gruff voice at the other end. "You didn't notify me about that gun as you promised."

The sergeant did not attempt to make an apology. His voice was low and reluctant. "Oh, it's the murder weapon all right," he growled. "We're turning it over to the prosecutor as exhibit number one!"

The minister's voice did not reveal his relief and joy. "Oh, I see! Then our lawyer can use it as evidence in the trial?"

"I suppose so! Is that all? I'm a busy man, you know!"

"Yes, thank you! Good-by!"

Mr. Pendelton turned to this wife and his eyes shone. "You heard what I said? It's the weapon Tarzan used to kill the merchant, all right! Now, there're only two things we've got to do – one, get Jonah back to stand trial; two, get the prosecutor to give the lad a fair trial. He'll *have* to stand trial; he *was* with the crooks and that'll go against him."

"Do you think Jonah will be sent to prison?" Mrs. Pendelton's voice was anxious.

"It'll be too bad if he is. He'll be thrown amongst some of the worst *tsotsis* and other criminal types, and he'd have to be pretty strong spiritually to resist their brain-washing!"

"You mean if he wasn't a criminal when he went in he'd be one when he came out!"

The minister looked thoughtful. "You know, dear," he said. "In a way that 'Curse' Jonah is always fretting about may have been a blessing in disguise. It gives him something to worry about. He's never been able to throw it aside and enjoy life – so Gideon told me. So even in prison he might be set apart by his inward fear so as not to be keen to join in with others! Still, I'd do anything to prevent his serving a sentence."

"Yes, and there's Miriam! She's doing so well now she's with us – blossoming out at church, in the auxiliary, in the other groups. She seems to think a lot of Jonah. Although I don't see how that can be, seeing she only saw him the once, for such a short time, too."

"Perhaps it's love at first sight, dear."

Mr. Pendelton looked at the clock. "I was going to make an early start for Rhodesia," he said. "It's now ten o'clock! I hope Mr. Webster has been able to contact Jonah – that is, if the boy is still there. He seems to be on the run the whole time. You're sure you'll be all right alone, dear?"

"You forget; I have Miriam! I'd like to come with you but this bazaar's too near. You go now and enjoy yourself. I'll pray for your services."

"Do that, dear." And the pastor kissed his wife on the cheek as he left.

12

JONAH HAD WORKED a week at the gasoline storage depot. It was not easy work. The trucks had to be unloaded quickly; their drivers could not stay long. So the "unloaders," stripped to the waist, sweated and struggled with the heavy drums. Jonah did not mind the night work. It gave him a chance to walk about the city in the daytime, seeing the wonders of Rhodesia. He got home soon after eight in the morning and slept till noon. Then he felt rested enough to get up, wash, have breakfast, and go for a walk. He had paid the jolly African girl what he owed her and enough to keep his room for another week. He went to his night shift happy to be out of debt and to have a few coins to jingle in his pocket. The work went well that night. The *baas* even went so far as to say, "You're not a bad worker. Better'n some of them lazy bums!"

Jonah whistled as he walked cheerily toward his room. He was thinking of what he'd have for breakfast. "Think I'll try some American cereal," he murmured. He pushed open the door and stopped short. A man sat insolently on his bed. In his mouth was a big cigar. His suit was bright blue. He wore a high collar and a big yellow tie. His hands rested on the handle of a walking stick. It was Judas Balatwa! The sight of his gold teeth repulsed Jonah.

His knees felt suddenly weak. He swallowed hard. The bottom had dropped out of his world. Judas' harsh laugh did not make him feel any better. "You look like a fish on a slab of ice!" he said coarsely.

Jonah sat down abruptly. "What . . . what do you want?" His voice was weak, like the old Jonah. Again Judas laughed. Then his face grew stern. He leaned forward and his voice sounded like the hiss of the snake.

"So . . . you made a mess of it, eh? You had to lose the money our dear *baas,* Mr. Kwanda, gave you from his hard earned supply!" He banged his stick on the floor with a sharp sound that made Jonah jump. "Do you know he is in prison? All because of you? That packet of money – fingerprints. You *mompara!"*

Jonah ducked the swinging walking stick. "I could – not help it, sir!" he said. "It . . . it was done in the excitement of crossing——"

"Stop! Enough stammering! What's done is done. But——" an evil, self-satisfied smile creased his face. "Things might be worse. *I* am carrying on the great work!" He sat up straight and struck his chest. "Yes! Me . . . Judas Balatwa. I am leader! Lucky *I* was not arrested, eh? I am too smart for them." Jonah had not reckoned on Kwanda having a successor. He had hoped to escape the tyranny of these Communists with Kwanda's capture.

Again Judas leaned toward the shaking youth. "I hear you are working at the petrol storage place. Right?" Jonah nodded. He stared like one held spellbound by the glare of the witch doctor. How had this man come into his life again? Just when he had begun to find a new happiness and a peace he had not known. How had Judas learned about the place where he worked? What use was it to struggle against this diabolical power that seemed to follow him like an evil spirit? Could he never escape the Curse? So Jonah sat, feeling as small and helpless as a mouse.

Judas blew a great puff of blue smoke and stood up. "What a stinking little room you got, Jonah!" he said, and spat in his contempt. "If you go along with us you'll have lots of money. You'll live in a real house. Oh, they're helping in Rhodesia, too! Look at this!" He pulled a newspaper out of his pocket, found a paragraph, and shoved it in front of Jonah's face. Jonah read the headline: "BOMB THROWN IN CAFE; NINE INJURED."

"I have heard of that," he said.

"Oh, you did? But read on; read *that* part!" A fat finger indicated another paragraph. "Chief Inspector Maxwell identified the fragments of the hand grenade found at the scene of the crime as of Russian origin . . . ."

"You see, if we play our cards right the Soviets will send us unlimited funds and supplies! Yes – Russia and China! Who do you suppose trained all these guerilla fighters, these chaps who are doing such a splendid work blowing up bridges, disrupting traffic, burning down homes and killing the White farmers and their families? Our friends, the Reds, of course!" His laugh reminded Jonah of the hyena that had trailed him in the jungle. He felt just as hounded.

"Yes, I do work at the petrol dump, but I . . .I———" (It took a lot of courage–) "I am not going to do anything bad . . . ."

Judas towered above him. The crook of his stick was around Jonah's neck. His face came down close to Jonah's. Smoke from his mouth made the youth's eyes smart. "You'll do as we say!" Judas hit the youth in the stomach.

Jonah dropped to his knees, gasping for air while Judas sat again on the bed. "This is the plan. I know where to get more of these grenades. I shall bring them to you. What time do you go to work, and what time do you leave?"

Jonah was breathing easier now and found the pain not unbearable. He resolved to keep still. At least he could show that much bravery. *I can take his punches,* he thought.

But Judas reached out his long stick again and the pain of it striking the back of his neck made flashes of light come before Jonah's eyes. His resolve was shattered. "All right . . . I'll talk!"

Judas laughed again. "What a brave man you are!"

Jonah's voice was small and angry. "I go in at midnight and work until eight."

"Good! Just before you go off duty – or even as you go out – you simply toss a grenade or two into the center of the tins of petrol. See?"

Jonah stood up. A wave of horror swept over him. "But what will happen? I will lose my job . . . ."

Judas doubled up at the stupidity of the statement. "There won't *be* any job when the gas is gone," he chuckled. "Don't worry!

There's plenty more work for you to do. When are you going to Zambia? And when do you see the Lion?"

Jonah had almost forgotten the hated name. He sat silent. Life was like that. One moment the sun shone, the birds sang. The next, thunder and lightning, the howl of the tempest. Despair. But in the midst of his misery – like the voice of a tiny bird cheeping in the center of the storm – came a small sound in his heart. "Blessed are ye when men shall revile you . . . ." But none of this inward hope showed in his face. He was helpless in the presence of the great Judas Balatwa, with his stick, his cigar and his gold teeth.

"Now memorize this, my boy." Judas threw the butt of his cigar on the floor and lit another, speaking between puffs as it was being lit. "When you go to Zambia – right after you set fire to the dump – you will go to Livingstone Street, in Lusaka. Got that?" The cigar was lit now and the smoke clouded the small room. "There you will find the office of the *Zambian Clarion*. Yes, the set-up is much like we had in Johannesburg." He bent forward, menacingly. "The nice set-up you had to go and spoil for us, eh *mompara!* You know the password? No need for me to repeat it. There, if you're lucky, you'll see the Lion. Listen carefully to all he tells you. He's a mighty man. He'll bring about the downfall of the Whites in our land, if I know anything. I'd go up and do the job, but" – he flourished the cigar airily – "I have more important business to attend to."

Jonah sat miserably wondering if it were a bad dream. "Then you go to Kenya! You'll have a job to get across the borders of these lands. You just might get a few bullets in your back, but" – again that incessant laugh – "it's all in a good cause. There you'll see the man who calls himself the 'Cannibal.' " He paused. "A good name, eh? More than a name, too, if we can believe all we hear! Learn this off by heart, too. We can't put anything down in writing. Too dangerous." He looked round and lowered his voice. "He's a lawyer and his office is on Stanley Street in Nairobi. You'll see his name – not 'Cannibal' – his real name, Mr. Thomas Kundu. Got that? Now, to see if your brain is not dead, repeat what I've told you."

Jonah, like a zombie and in a voice equally dead, said slowly, "I find the Lion" – a pause – "at the Clarion office on Livingstone Street in Lusaka in Zambia. And Mr. Kundu on Stanley Street, Nairobi. He is known as" – another pause – "the 'Cannibal.' "

"Not bad! Not bad! You're not as stupid as I thought you were! You go to work at twelve tonight, right? I'll be here by eleven or so" – again his face drew level with Jonah's and his voice came like the hiss of the mamba – "with the hardware you will need. And, Hyena, if you fail me——" He and Tarzan were both fond of that gesture, a finger drawn across the throat. Jonah felt physically sick.

After Judas had gone Jonah closed the door and threw himself on the bed. Despair went through him like a fever. How wrong he had been to think that he could be happy, even for a few days! He had been like the foolish *blesbok,* dancing happily on the veld while the lion skulked in the bushes nearby, biding his time, then leaping out with crushing power on the stupid animal.

But Jonah was learning something. His shocking experiences had taught him that he was not alone in his misery. If the Nkulunkulu had come to his help in the jungle, across the river, in the cities, surely He would help him now!

Jonah lay there thinking. He had several alternatives. He could go through with Judas' mad scheme; or he could go to the police and tell them what was afoot. That would mean letting them know who he was and would result in arrest and being sent back to South Africa. The thought of going back and facing the White Judge and White Jury was appalling. Or perhaps he could run away. As Jonah recalled his wanderings across the sun-baked veld, amid the jungle, with the beasts of the field, he knew that was not the answer. What a position to be in! Every way he looked he was trapped. All he could do was pray; this was one time when a man's brain could think of nothing else.

Out of nowhere an idea flashed into Jonah's mind. *I shall go to church!* He had seen, as he passed to and from work, a sign outside the little church in the *Location.* It spoke about daily Lenten services and invited all to worship the Lord and to meditate on the Crucifixion and Resurrection.

But services were not until two o'clock; time for a sleep. Somehow Jonah felt his heart grow lighter after he had made that decision. Miracles had happened before in his turbulent life; perhaps they would happen again. He remembered a verse of the Good Book. *How strange,* he thought, *that these verses I thought I had forgotten are coming back to me now when I need their help and comfort most.* "Call upon Me in the day of trouble. I will deliver thee and thou shalt glorify Me . . . ." Jonah fell asleep just as he lay. It was one o'clock when he awoke.

He was hungry. All thoughts of breakfast had been driven from his mind by the unwelcome visit of Judas Balatwa. He washed, then walked across to the cafe for a good feed. The happy waitress pushed a plateful of soup toward him. "You don't look so good," she said. "Since you got that job you been very happy. You lost it maybe?"

Jonah tried to smile. He did not know his face showed his feelings. "No, I still have my job. I feel fine!" The girl shook her head. Jonah took his plate and moved over to a table. He did not want to talk with the girl. The way he felt she might easily reach into his heart and take out all that he knew.

At two o'clock Jonah made his way to the church. He sat down near the back. The place was not full, but those who were there were women. Most of the men were at work. A white pastor, in his robes, followed by an African – also robed – came in from the back and bowed in prayer at the altar. The native, first in one language, then in another, spoke of the purpose of the services and said how happy he was to welcome the Reverend Samuel Webster, who was giving the address today.

Then the African announced the hymn. "When I survey the wondrous cross . . . ."

Jonah was glad of his mission experience. He was able to join in the singing and to understand the words. As he sang he could see Ujesu Kristu – the Saviour of the Black Man as well as the White. Jonah saw Him hanging on that cross and somehow his own sufferings faded away as he saw

> ". . . from His head, His hands, His feet,
> Sorrow and love flow mingled down . . . ."

And when the last verse was sung Jonah agreed with all his being that "love so amazing, so divine" demanded his soul, his life, his all. For the first time in his life – although he had made feeble attempts while still at home – Jonah wanted to give himself, body, soul and mind to this Saviour. He had tried to do it in Zululand, but the evil influence of Madadikto was too strong, his father's wrath too powerful to resist. Now Jonah felt free from all that; even the Curse seemed to be losing its grip on his soul. He was glad he had come to the church. It had done one thing for him – it had made him realize that his own agony, however intense, was as nothing compared to that of *Ujesu Kristu.*

All through the service–prayers, offering, hymns and sermon– Jonah was like one in a dream. *Oh, if I could only stay here always,* he said to himself. *Away from the hard battle of life; away from scheming, wicked men, men who only think of money and power;*

men who think the knife or the gun are the only things that can settle problems; men who like to use their power to make weaker ones do wrong – do their evil deeds for them and then get away when the blow falls. But no! I must go back . . .

Mr. Webster spoke in a way that all could understand – even the children who had come with their mothers. A few men and boys straggled in during the service and all seemed very attentive. The pastor made the Bible story sound as though it had happened today, right in Rhodesia! Jonah could see *Kristu* "stedfastly set His face to go to Jerusalem" – even though He knew it would mean the most savage of deaths, being nailed to a wooden cross in full view of great crowds of people. Jonah could see Him standing before the crafty High Priest, a man mad with jealousy because this upstart had gained so much popularity with the people. His hands were tied with ropes that cut into the flesh. Mr. Webster spoke of those bonds. "Those hands which had done so much good – healing and soothing – they tied them fast, so that he could not use them."

Jonah could see *Kristu* before Pilate, still calm and loving in spite of the humiliation. He heard the multitude screaming "Crucify Him; release unto us Barabbas" and flinched as the cruel whip brought the blood across the back of the Victim. Jonah had never heard the story told so tenderly and vividly. He marveled as he heard the words *Ujesu* spoke to those women on the way to the cross, "Weep not for Me, but for yourselves . . . ." And how, even on the cross itself, He had forgotten His own sufferings and had thought of His mother, and had actually asked God's forgiveness for the men who had driven the spikes through His hands.

"I think you will all agree that if you owned the whole world and could give it to God, 'that would be a present far too small.' " In closing he urged all present to "forget the bitterness of the present times! The injustices will all be solved in time. But be ruled in all your dealings with your own or with the Whites by the love of God, the 'love that enabled Jesus to endure the cross, despising the shame . . . .' "

Jonah kept his head bowed for a few moment after the African parson had pronounced the benediction. When he got up to go out the women and all the others had filed past him and were shaking hands with the two clergymen at the door.

The white man took his hand in a firm clasp and asked him who he was. "Are you new to this place?" Jonah's heart beat, as it always did when anyone sought to know his identity.

"I am" – he almost said Joseph Panzani, but didn't. He said, "I am Jonah Umlungu, and I would like to speak with you."

The white parson took his hand and held it while he looked right into Jonah's eyes. Jonah felt his legs growing weak again. "What – why do you . . . look at me like that, Mfundisi?" he said, uncertainly.

"Come in here, my boy," said the minister. He led the way to a room near the door. "Sit down!" Jonah obeyed mechanically.

Mr. Webster looked right into Jonah's eyes. "So . . . you are Jonah Umlungu."

Jonah bowed his head. What could he say?

"Ah, then I was right! As I saw you right at the back sitting quietly and looking so forlorn, it flashed through my mind that you must be the youth Mr. Pendelton – ah, I see you know the name – wrote to me about a few days ago. He is coming up to do my Easter services for me, but he wrote and said if I should happen across you I was to speak to you."

The tears were falling now. Jonah felt that he had found a true friend. And at last he could let the walls of his heart crumble and could cry. Perhaps this was the way Nkulunkulu was answering his prayer. Maybe this man would find a solution to the awful predicament he was in. "Yes, I am Jonah Umlungu, and I would that I had never been born! The Cursed One, I am called!"

Then he remembered the vow he had made in the church only a few minutes before and was ashamed. "But God has been good to me. I was greatly stirred in the service today!" He felt better. He told the parson of his desire to give himself to *Ujesu Kristu*.

It was a short but simple effort. The two prayed as the youth confessed his wrong and asked the Great-Great to forgive him. He asked *Ujesu Kristu* to come and live inside him and make him over. The two rose.

Mr. Webster looked at the lad with eyes full of pity. "Mr. Pendelton told me something of your story, my boy," he said. "He believes in your innocence and is doing all he can to help you. You mustn't give way to despair. Now, tell me, just what are you doing in Salisbury? What are your plans for the future?"

Jonah sat silent. *How much shall I tell him?* he thought. *I can see this man is a true friend, but his advice will be the same as that of other White Men in my life – give yourself up to the police. That means being taken back to the Rand and facing a trial. Yet if I do not tell someone about tonight I am forced to do a terrible wrong and perhaps kill someone. Oh, Ujesu! I need Your strong power very much,* he prayed.

The native pastor came to the door of the room. Mr. Webster looked up. "Amos, I'll tell you about this lad afterward. Would you mind leaving us for the moment? I'll make my own way back to the manse in my car. Thanks for your help. I felt it was a successful service!"

Amos smiled, looked at Jonah, then walked off. Jonah heard the door close. They were alone. What should he say? How much of his miserable story should he reveal.

"You can trust me, Jonah," said the parson, gently. "I suppose you are afraid I will report your presence here to the police. Rest assured, I don't think it is necessary. But come, let us go to my home. There we can discuss the whole thing."

Jonah rose. No harm could come of that, he thought. On the way to the city he could think of what he should say.

Mr. Webster reached for his hat, took off his robe, folded it, placed it in a satchel and said, "I'm ready! Let's go!"

13

MR. WEBSTER LED THE WAY out to the car and opened the door for Jonah to get in. The parson got in the driver's seat, slammed his door shut and started the car. As they rounded the corner into the street their progress was hindered for a moment by a crowd of boys and girls crossing the road from the school. Men and women were walking about the Location. Jonah's heart sank. Among them was an insolent, swaggering figure, dressed in his bright blue suit, and as always, puffing a cigar. It was Judas Balatwa! Jonah tried to shrink back in the car but it was small and did not provide much room to hide. Their eyes met. Balatwa's widened – first in surprise, then in anger. His mouth also fell open. The car started again and Jonah sank back in relief. But he had seen enough in Judas' puffy eyes to convince him that the man was far from pleased.

Mr. Webster did not sense Jonah's discomfort and talked of many things as the car rolled along. But he did not discuss Jonah's plans. As they neared the University he slowed up. A great crowd swarmed around the gates of the building and overflowed onto the road and the grounds. Shouts and screams were heard, even a block away.

"Ah, just what I feared," said the minister.

"What is going on?" asked Jonah.

"Riots, my boy. Riots! You may not know much about our problems here but we have plenty! Since Ian Smith declared what we call 'Unilateral Independence' there has been violence. He has broken away from England's power over the land. He knew Britain wanted all the Africans to have the vote and he thought it would mean, and it would, of course, sweeping the White Man out of the country. And much more is to follow, I'm afraid."

"But what have these students to do with it?"

"Well, you know students all over the world are the most aggressive when it comes to sizing up a situation. And they don't stop at *thinking* about it. They act! Haven't you seen pictures in the papers of students carrying signs, protesting over something or other?"

Jonah nodded.

The clergyman was turning his car. "I must go another way," he said. "This university was quite an experiment. We have both Blacks and Whites here. Now you can see how differences of opinion would arise among them. But the real trouble is caused by the professors. Some of them are from other countries – America, Canada, and South Africa. The Americans, especially, are strongly in favor of the Africans having the vote – 'One man, one vote' is the motto."

Jonah looked back as the car turned off the street on which the university stood. He could see the downward sweep of strong arms, with placards and clubs flashing in the sunshine. Figures rolled over in the gutter; Black chased White and White chased Black. To Jonah it all seemed so unnecessary.

"There'll have to be a clean-up after this," said the rector, sadly. "I happen to be one of the directors of the University. It's sad, but I'm afraid that the professors who stick up for the Black students will be turned out."

The streets were strangely deserted, although it was afternoon, and the sun was bright. Police cars glided silently along the streets. On the sidewalks armed men paraded. Jonah caught glimpses of anxious faces peering from windows. *How will it all end?* he thought. *Will this terrible "blood bath" that the witch doctors–of both races–have predicted come to pass?* It was hard to believe that they were sitting on the top of a volcano. All looked so peaceful. The blossoming trees seemed so gay; the lawns, trimmed hedges, flower gardens were so neat and tidy. Jonah knew that as long as men refused to look upon everyone as brothers there would be strife.

"Here we are!" The clergyman turned into a driveway that led to a garage, built at the back of a roomy bungalow, and stopped the car.

"This way, my boy!" Jonah followed him up the front steps and into the house. The parson pointing to a room on the right said, "Sit there!" and disappeared. Jonah trod carefully on the carpet and sat gingerly in an easy chair. A square polished box stood in the corner of the room. The front of it consisted of a square of glass and he stared in amazement. Practically the same scene he had just witnessed was taking place – in a small way – on the glass before him. But the scene was without color and did not seem real. Jonah heard a man's voice coming out of the box. He had never seen television. It was not allowed in South Africa. The government, strongly Dutch Reformed Church and Puritan, felt it would corrupt the young people. Even if it had been in existence he would not have seen it, except maybe in store windows. The voice was saying, "We understand riots are taking place at the University of Rhodesia. These are films made in February when similar riots broke out. It is believed the police have the problem well in hand. However, residents are urged to remain in their homes and not clutter up the streets adjacent to the riots. From a reliable source we are assured that those responsible for the outbreak of trouble are to be strictly dealt with."

The minister entered the room, followed by a cheerful looking woman. "This is Mrs. Webster, my boy. This is Jonah Umlungu!"

The lady shook his hand. "I left the TV on, I see. I'll turn it off so we can talk." She crossed the room, turned a button and the picture faded. Jonah still stared in amazement at the magic box. This was another of the White Man's wonders. Truly there was no end to them.

"We'd like you to stay to tea with us, Jonah," said the minister's wife, brightly. "We have a student coming, David Ubangi; that is, if the riots will let him! Make yourself at home. You will stay, won't you? Sit down!"

Jonah had stood as soon as the lady came into the room. Now he sat, feeling a little awkward. Mr. Webster excused himself. "Have to do a spot of work in my study. I'll be right back!"

"You must have had a terrible time getting up here, if what I hear is true," said Mrs. Webster. "By the way, are you working? Have you time to stay awhile?"

Jonah found he was able to talk, although he felt shy. "Yes, I have a job at the petrol storage place. But I–I–don't have to go until midnight!"

The minister's wife stood once more. "I'll get afternoon tea," she said. "Sam always like a cup when he comes in from the afternoon service." She went out and Jonah was left with his thoughts.

The word "midnight" recalled the unpleasantness of the morning. Perhaps it would be better if he sneaked out and ran. He always seemed to be on the run. Never able to settle down and enjoy life. Run, run, run. It would be easy for him to tiptoe to the door, open it softly and dart out into the street. But where would he go? The thought of taking to the jungle again made him scared. Besides, why run away from kindness? These Christian White people were good to Black men. No other White Man would invite you into his home to have tea. They might show you their servants' shed in the backyard and curtly tell you to go there, but in their front parlors – never! So ran Jonah's thoughts. It was almost impossible to get away from the eternal problem of Black versus White in this land. He had heard, though, that the problem existed in other lands as well. America, for instance. But he knew very little about that.

Soon, with a tiny jingle of crockery, Mrs. Webster came in and set the tray on a small table and then sat down herself. "This is our maid's day off, Jonah," she said. "But I like doing a bit of housework myself. And making tea is a real art, don't you think?"

Jonah felt rather foolish. Tea-drinking is not too common among the Zulus.

Mr. Webster came in and the three sat drinking tea and nibbling the biscuits Mrs. Webster had set out. Jonah's shyness was evident. This was the first time he could remember having food in the home of a White Man. He felt clumsy, and in trying to avoid spilling his tea, he knocked a cookie onto the floor. He apologized and picked it up. Mrs. Webster laughed. "Don't worry about that, my boy! Now, I expect you two have a lot to say to one another so I'll go. Got to get the supper on!"

"Now, Jonah," said the cleric, when his wife had gone. "You don't have to tell me your story unless you want to. But I am sure I can help you. It's only the fact that we have heavy troubles of our own right now that is preventing our police from raising a hue and cry after you – this 'desperate murderer, who broke away from custody' as the newspapers have put it. Now I know that description is not true. Mr. Pendelton believes you are taking the blame for a crime one of your companions committed. Isn't that right?"

Jonah nodded, sadly. "But the police do not believe that. They have already judged me. I am a dead man!"

"Don't say that. If evidence comes to light that proves your innocence they will have to let you go. First of all, are you working here?"

Jonah told the minister about his job. "And you're staying at the Location? Now here's an idea. Why not return to South Africa——" Jonah jumped up in alarm. "Sit down! Not in a police van." Mr. Webster laughed. "But with Mr. Pendelton. He's due here any time now, probably tomorrow. He could take you back with him and keep you in his home – or somewhere safe – until you have been able to prove that you are not guilty of this crime. He tells me you have a good native lawyer and a minister who has promised to help you? What have you got to lose?"

He stopped and looked expectantly at Jonah. The youth sat for a long time, hands tightly clasped in his uncertainty. Then Jonah made up his mind.

He stood again, his face working in his distress. "Mfundisi, I'm in terrible trouble. I'm ordered to blow up the dump tonight!" He sank onto the couch, his head buried in his hands.

Mr. Webster was at his side in a moment, hand on his shoulder. "What is all this, my boy? Are you telling the truth?"

Jonah told him the whole story. At the end, he said brokenly, "You see why I cannot go back with Mr. Pendelton? They would kill me! They made me take an oath that I would not break faith with them – that I would do everything they wanted me to do! It's true Mr. Kwanda is in prison but Mr. Balatwa is not. And he will never stop following my trail until I am dead!"

The minister stood looking down at the boy's hopeless pose for a long time. He had known something of the hatred and fierce lust for revenge that existed, but this was worse than he had imagined. He had also suspected that the Communists were at the bottom of the trouble; or at least, in their well-known manner, scenting trouble, they add wood to the fire until the flames mount high.

Jonah raised his tired and fear-stained face. "If you could have seen him this afternoon when he saw me in your car, Mfundisi——"

The pastor had sat down, but he rose quickly. "You say he saw you riding away with me in the car? Why, then, you can stop worrying! You don't think for one moment he'll go through with this mad scheme if he knows you have been consorting with White people! Did he look angry – suspicious?"

Jonah sat back and wiped his face. "He looked – what you say – flabbergasted? And angry at the same time. I think you right, Mfundisi. He will be afraid to bring those bombs to me for fear we may set a trap and catch him." Jonah's face brightened. "But he won't stop there, Mfundisi!" His fear had returned. "It will make him angrier than ever against me. He will find me and . . . ." His voice trailed off weakly.

Mr. Webster paced the floor, his face wrinkled in thought. "I know the obvious thing is to go to the police and tell them about this monstrous plot, but I'm afraid that will involve you. Besides, I doubt whether he will stay here. Don't you think that, as soon as he saw you in my car, the thought would run through his mind that you were on the way to inform the police?"

Again Jonah looked hopeful. "Perhaps you're right, Mfundisi! He would think the police would begin to hunt for him right away and he'd go into hiding!"

Mr. Webster excused himself and left the room. He returned with Mrs. Webster. "We both feel you should not return to that room of yours, my boy. Balatwa may leave town, or he may go into hiding, just to take his revenge on you. My wife wants you to come to us for the time being. I still think you could return to the south with Mr. Pendelton but we'll talk about that later. There won't be room for you in the house itself, as we'll be having the minister as a guest, but there's a very clean little place at the back. We had a boy, as gardener, but he's away visting his people in Nyasaland. You're welcome to stay there."

A great weight lifted from Jonah's breast. "I'd be very glad, Mfundisi."

Mrs. Webster's face was like sunshine. "And you'll eat with us, of course! We'll have Mr. Pendelton, too, and we can discuss your future. Right?"

Jonah was nervous. He started as the doorbell rang. Mrs. Webster went to the door and Jonah – half rising from his chair in his fear – heard an African voice. He sat down again. Mrs. Webster came in with a well-dressed young native and introduced him as David Ubangi. Jonah felt humbled in the presence of this fine student. David was a man of book learning and culture, yet he shook hands heartily and put Jonah at ease. Mrs. Webster returned to her kitchen duties.

"Again I'll have to excuse myself," said the pastor. "The work seems endless! But you two have a good chat! I know you'll get along well together."

Jonah was shy at first. He had always envied his brother Africans who could afford a higher education than he himself had. But David was very friendly. He expected to become a minister and was a Christian in every way. To look down on anyone because he was not so fortunate as he was – no! That was not David Ubangi! David was drawn to this travel-worn African, who seemed to carry fear in his eyes. There was an air of mystery about Jonah that he could not define.

After awhile tongues that had been stiff with shyness became loosened. Jonah felt he had never had a more interesting hour than the one he spent with David in Mr. Webster's front room. He found himself asking endless questions about college life. David generated a desire in the heart of the fugitive to be a student; to read many books, and to enter into the minds of great men who had put their thoughts into print to enrich men and women of following generations.

The talk came round to the rioting. David waved his hand. "I don't get mixed up in it," he said. "There are a lot of hot heads who think they are helping the cause of *Uhuru* by carrying signs and throwing bombs [Jonah started, but David did not seem to notice] and listening to every rabble-rouser who can get up on a soapbox."

"The Mfundisi said some of the professors were a bit rash?"

David stretched out his long legs and put his hands behind his head. "True! You see, they have not lived in Africa long enough to understand the problems. They think it's a simple matter to give the vote to everybody – educated and ignorant, rich and poor alike. They are fond of saying 'Africa for the Africans,' but while I am as anxious as anybody to see our people govern themselves I realize that we owe a lot to the White People. Who built our fine roads, our dams, our bridges? Look at that Kariba dam. Why, that will make millions of acres able to grow food, land that had been like a desert before!"

"What do the other students think of your attitude?"

David smiled; it was a little sad. "Oh, the other Africans? Some of them hate me for it! It's not easy. I come back into my room and find letters . . . or my things spilled out on the floor. Oh, I don't mind it so much; nothing terrible has happened. Besides, I'm there to get an education – not to make friends and find a social life. These people are kind to me. I spend most of my free time here– or with our African pastor at the Location. You see, I'm going to be a minister!"

Jonah was overawed at supper-time. To sit at a table spread with a white cloth, shining silver knives and forks, gleaming cups and saucers, and lovely food was something quite new to him. He watched David out of the corners of his eyes to see how he acted, and then did the same. He saw that the student unfolded a small cloth that lay at the side of his plate and spread it over his knees. Jonah did the same. He noticed what spoon David used for his soup, and what knife and fork he used for his other courses, and he did likewise. His hosts, if they noticed his embarrassment, did their best to make him happy, and the conversation was bright and cheerful.

"Everybody had enough?" said Mr. Webster at last. All nodded. He reached to the sideboard and picked up a Bible, with a worn and cracked cover. "Must have a promise from the Word," he smiled. "We're up to the 31st." Mrs. Webster and the two Africans settled back in their chairs, and the parson began to read:

> *"In Thee, O Lord, do I put my trust; never let me be ashamed . . . . Pull me out of the net that they have laid privily for me: for Thou art my strength . . . I have hated them that regarded lying vanities: but I trust in the Lord . . . I am forgotten as a dead man . . . My times are in Thy hand: deliver me from the hand of mine enemies . . . ."*

Jonah sat like one in a trance. It was just as though David had written this portion of Scripture with him in mind! Every verse seemed to contain a reference to him and his troubles. *"Let the lying lips be put to silence . . . ."* Even that found an echo in his heart, for had he not been lied about by those who wanted to crush him? The last verse made his eyes bright with hope. He heard the minister read, *"Be of good courage, and he shall strengthen your heart, all ye that hope in the Lord."*

Oh, if he could only keep always in the spirit of that verse! To be brave; to drive away fear; to have hope – at all times – even when things looked blackest! He would try; he had enough experience now of God's goodness to him to believe that He wanted to help him. He would try!

The minister prayed that God would bless the two young Africans, youths placed in such widely differing circumstances, and help them to witness for the Lord. He also prayed for the Easter services and for the peace of the country that was experiencing so much strife.

Afterward he said: "Jonah, you'll need to get your things from your room if you are going to stay with us. I'll take you now if you like!"

"I'll be gone by the time you return so we'd better say good-by now," said David. Jonah shook hands and the youths looked into each others' eyes. Mr. Webster, as he looked at the two Africans, thought, *The future of the land will be safe if men like these two have anything to do with it.* He had faith in Jonah. He felt the lad had had a bad start in life, but that, with proper training, he might do well.

Mr. Webster said little as they drove through the darkness toward the Location. As they drew near, and Jonah remembered what had happened the last time he had pushed open the door of his room, he shivered. The pastor noticed his movement.

"Much has happened since your early morning visitor, eh, Jonah?" he said. "I think you can go in there now without any fear. He'll keep his distance for fear of a trap, I'm thinking!"

Even so, it was with an eerie feeling that Jonah turned the handle of his door and gave it a shove. He wanted to make it short. The place was hateful to him now. He could sense the presence of the gross Mr. Balatwa; the smell of his cigar still hung about the room. Jonah could see his grinning, gold-toothed face as vividly as though the man were in the room. He reached for his knapsack which held his belongings and then he saw it! Just a piece of wood on the bed, but it made his heart beat faster. He picked it up with a hand that shook. "Ka – ka – *Kalolozi* gun!" he stuttered.

He sank on to a chair, in a half faint, shaking from head to foot. The little stick of wood was carved to represent a man. One hand was raised as though pointing. Balatwa, overly-dressed in the White Man's fashion, was yet steeped in all the superstitions of his race. He had evidently armed himself with this sinister symbol. The innocent looking doll was a *"kalolozi gun"* – aimed at a man, he would die. Jonah knew just the mere pointing of this simple little device was enough to bring death to a man or woman in the best of health! He had seen it happen. Balatwa had not been brave enough to stay and face Jonah and tax him with his apparent treachery in going to the White Man. Nor had he had a chance to point the "gun" at the lad; he had merely left it on the bed as a sign that he would remember; that his vengeance might be delayed but it would be sure.

Jonah could not move. He felt weak as water. He was young in the faith and did not know that the "good medicine" of *Ujesu Kristu* was strong enough to fight the Bad Medicine of the devil's agents. His experience that afternoon did not completely erase the influence of Madadikto. He had seen strange and awful wonders; he had seen men gradually shrink and die as a result of some such "weapon" as he now held in his hand. He had seen the effect of "love potions"– evil mixtures that, when drunk, would turn the heart of a man or woman. All these the White Man laughed at, yet they were real! He had seen some of these strange wonders in the jungle when Madadikto and his evil colleagues went through their rituals. He had heard weird voices coming out of nowhere. He had actually seen rain come at the command of the devil dancers!

The door opened and Mr. Webster came in. "Come on, Jonah, we've – why, whatever is the matter? You look as though you've seen a ghost or something! I say . . . what's that? Why it's only one of those homemade dolls from the native villages. I've seen dozens of 'em!"

Jonah made a big effort and stood to his feet. "I . . . I'm sorry, Mfundisi! I am weak – a coward. I, who gave myself to the Lord today, to be knocked over by . . . *this*––" He shuddered. "B-but it is evil, *baas!* It is a 'kalolozi gun.' It will kill!"

The pastor snatched the thing from Jonah's hand, and shoved it into his pocket. "Nonsense! Don't give way to these silly superstitions! This is simply a bit of wood. If you want to ascribe to its demonic properties, that's up to you! To me it's a doll – fit for a child to play with, nothing more!"

Jonah only understood half of what he said, but he was still trembling as he picked up his knapsack, and slipped into it the few articles on the dresser or in the drawers.

"I must go to pay for my room, Mfundisi," he said. "I come in a minute!"

"All right! I'll wait for you in the car. Don't be long! I have a service tonight!"

Jonah stepped like one in a dream as he made his way through the beer hall to the counter. The place was full of noisy, drinking, laughing Africans. He looked around, half expecting to see Judas there, but on second thought he knew that was the last place Balatwa would show his face. He suspected that Jonah had gone right to the police about his plot to blow up the petrol dump, and the beer hall would be the first place the police would look for him.

The girl, Debra, again noticed Jonah's discomfort. "I told you that you didn't look good this morning," she said. "You look even worse now! What's the matter? You can trust me!"

Jonah looked at her gratefully. So many people had befriended him; if only he could open his heart to them and tell them all, but he could not. This hateful secret he carried about with him prevented him from being a normal person and making friends readily.

"I want to thank you for your kindness to me," he said. "And to tell you I am giving up my room. I–I–have another place to go to!"

The girl looked at him keenly. "Oh, a better place, I suppose? We're not good enough for you, no? You were glad to come begging——"

Jonah was confused. He could not explain where he was going to stay and why. Then he saw she was only teasing. Her happy smile shone out again and she said: "You don't have to tell me! We have folk coming and going all the time here! Let's see, you owe me——" She quickly figured up Jonah's debts, he paid and walked swiftly through the crowd to the car. One or two Africans clapped him on the shoulder as he passed – they had got to know this quiet stranger a little – but no one stopped him.

Mr. Webster was examining the *"kalolozi* gun" when Jonah came up to the car. Jonah began to tremble again. "Please, Mfundisi, put that thing away. It makes me feel frightened. I know I shouldn't be, but——"

Mr. Webster laughed and again thrust the doll into his pocket. "I'll burn it in the yard incinerator when I get home, Jonah. That'll be the end of that foolishness."

"No, you mustn't burn it, Mfundisi!" Jonah's face was full of fear. "It – is Bad Medicine! If you burn it, it will bring calamity on your whole household and – and – perhaps you will die!"

Mr. Webster had not yet started the car. "Do you really believe that?" He looked long and hard at the shivering lad. Jonah did not know what to say. "Please, sir," he began, "you must think I'm foolish, but–but–I–my father made me live with a Medicine Man when I was young——"

"Oh, now I'm beginning to see daylight. I can quite see why you have an unreasonable dread of these diabolical symbols, but I can also see that you want to do right. You seem to want to break free from the shackles of superstition. Did you stay with this – devil doctor all the time?"

"Oh, no, Mfundisi! I did not like it at all, and I got many beatings from my father because I ran to the mission school. Mfundisi Beckwith was so good to me. He tried to sweep away the evil cobwebs that Madadikto had put there, but the spider still remained! But it did stop me from becoming – well, from turning into a full-time witch doctor. I have much to thank God for!"

"H'mm, quite."

The parson started the car, and drove slowly through the dark streets. He was thinking deeply about what Jonah had told him. It was easy for him, steeped in all the White Man's fearless way of life, brought up in the shadow of the Church, to laugh at the taboos and fetishes . . . the ugly little idols . . . the "throwing of the bones" . . . the "death-wish" . . . the magic potions – the whole rigmarole of black magic. But this youth was plunged into it from his boyhood, living in the unlighted jungle, with a man who was dedicated to the Devil. If he could show only a spark of faith in a wholesome, loving God, he was doing well.

"What do you propose we should do with this–this–thing?" he asked, as they drove into the manse driveway.

"Bury it, sir!" Jonah's voice was deep with earnestness. "Bury it tonight – and bury it deep down!"

"Well I never! Why it should be better to bury it than burn it, I'll never know. Still, you should know best. There's a shovel in that shed. But first, let me show you your room. Bring your things this way!"

There was a high hedge of privet around the back garden. In one corner stood the garage; in the other a shed – it was little better – with a door and a small window. Mr. Webster unlocked the door, handing the key to Jonah with a suggestion that he lock the door at night. He switched on the electric light – a bulb dangling from a wire – and pointed out the features of the place. "Your washroom is back by the hedge. It'll save you having to come into the house. I understand you go to work at midnight? And come back at eight. Well, you'll just be in time for breakfast inside with us, then you can go to your room, lock the door and sleep as long as you like; No doubt you'll want to get up at noon – or one – we usually have lunch at that time. You'll have lunch with us, then you can go back to sleep if you like. Just make yourself at home!"

Jonah stood looking at the minister with eyes shiny with tears. "Mfundisi, I can't think why——"

Mr. Webster held up his hand. "Don't try to thank me, my boy!

It's only a humble attempt to do what Christ told us we should do. Now, to the great interment! I mean, the burial! You be the gravedigger, I'll do the committal!"

Jonah was very solemn as he wielded the shovel. He made a hole fully two feet deep, and the minister stooped down and reverently placed the doll at the bottom. In feverish haste, Jonah shovelled the earth in. Sweat was pouring from his face as he did so, and it was not simply the heat of the evening that made him perspire. The minister noticed his fear and patted him on the shoulder. "I'll offer a special prayer for you when I go to bed, Jonah! That you may get complete victory over your horror of idols! Now, don't worry! You still have an hour or two before you have to go to work. Come on in the house! I saw you were interested in our TV. Haven't you seen it before? There's usually a good program at this time."

Jonah stood still. "But Mfundisi, I do not wish to – to make myself a nuisance. Perhaps your–uh–perhaps Mrs. Webster wants quiet––"

The pastor gently pushed Jonah toward the house. "Don't be silly! You can't sit out here doing nothing! By the way, I'll put a few books and magazines in your room to help you while away the hours when we're not at home, or when you can't sleep."

Mrs. Webster was seated in the front room darning socks when the two entered. "So you have brought your things from your room, right? You're sure you'll be all right in the room at the back? It's not very comfortable, but at least, it'll be quieter than the Location!" She laughed.

Jonah thanked her. They sat talking or watching TV, and again Jonah was thrilled by the magic of the big shiny box in the corner of the room. Mr. Webster liked cowboy stories, and Jonah gasped as the wiry horses galloped across the screen and the cowboys exchanged shots with the Indians. He could not help but feel that America had had its troubles with the native races in those far-off days. It did not matter how often the Indians raided the chuck-wagons and scalped the occupants, still the White Men kept on coming, until the prairies were studded with houses and churches and farms and ranches. Nothing could stop them. But then, the Indians were few in number. His own people numbered millions – two hundred million, someone had said.

Jonah rose to go about eleven o'clock, but Mrs. Webster stopped him. She put down her socks. "We always have a cup of coffee before going to bed. You'll feel better for a little. I won't be long!"

When it was time for him to go, they wished him well during his night duties. "It'll be different from your imaginings," said Mr. Webster. "Go in peace, son. And remember, God is with you. *Ujesu Kristu* lives within you. He will give you strength."

14

THE MOON WAS CLIMBING over the tops of the tall blue-gum trees as Jonah locked the door of his room, and set off for work. The street was a pattern of black and white. The dense shadows of the trees stretching from side to side of the road contrasted with the brilliant patches of moonlight between them. Although encouraged by the words of the parson and deriving strength from concentrating on the presence of *Ujesu Kristu* within, he was still not happy. He knew Balatwa lurked somewhere in that city. He might be following him now! A few minutes before he had felt safe in the well-lighted room of the Mfundisi. Watching the cowboys riding across the screen he had forgotten the dangers of the present time. He jumped as a cat darted out from the shadow of a jacaranda tree. He found himself trembling.

Why can't I be brave? he chided himself. *Where is my faith? What was it the Psalm had said: "Be of good courage, and He shall strengthen your heart . . . Hope in the Lord . . . ."*

David had no doubt composed those words when he was sitting watching his sheep, so Mfundisi Beckwith had explained one time. David had had his enemies. At that time they were the lion and the bear; later, evil men worked to bring about his downfall. But David had faith in God, and it kept him brave whether his foes were beasts or men. Jonah straightened and quickened his stride. *I will be brave like David!*

There were few cars out this night. Most people felt safer to stay indoors, especially after the rioting. The natives had to be off the streets. Headlights bore down on Jonah, the car stopped, and a lithe figure jumped out, shining a flashlight full into Jonah's face. The youth stopped short.

"Papers, boy, papers! What are you doing out this time of the night? Eh, answer me, answer me!"

Jonah could only stutter and stammer. But he had enough sense to pull out his papers, although his fingers were shaking so he could hardly open the pages. The officer snatched them away from him and shone his light on Jonah's passes. "Oh, you're working at the petrol storage place! Why didn't you say so, *mompara!* All right! You may go! But get there as fast as you can. Don't loiter or talk with other natives, hear?!"

Jonah nodded. He still could not speak. The White Police had a way of turning him into a rabbit. With unsteady fingers he folded his precious papers – his key to freedom – and thrust them into his pocket again.

But the White Police were not finished with him. The one officer had started to return to the car, when a voice came out of the darkened vehicle. "Ask him——" Jonah did not catch the rest of the question. The policeman seized him by the lapels of his coat. "What are you doing in this part of the town, eh? Answer me! You *skelm!* If you work at the storage depot you'd be staying at the Location. What are you doing here where only the White People live, eh?" He shook Jonah.

It was a full minute before Jonah could speak, the White Man was so aggressive. He managed to gasp out, "Mr. Webster, the Mfundisi. I stay at the back of his house!"

The man, still holding Jonah, turned to his partner. "Says he's staying at the parson's up the street. Shall be believe him?"

The other man got out of the car. "We could take him back there and question Webster, I suppose. Oh, I don't know! He looks a harmless sort of chap. And if he's late for work there'll be a stink, I guess. Let him go!"

The constable gave Jonah another final shove, for good measure, and said, "Off you go! If you've lied to us, woe betide you!"

The car moved off and Jonah stood trying to recover his wits. He had not thought, when he agreed to stay at the manse that it would lead to trouble like this. Truly, you never knew what was ahead in life. The Websters, too, had not realized that their guest would be suspected of roaming about illegally in a White district by inviting him to stay with them.

Jonah walked more quickly to his place of work. He had never been late, and he did not want to be late tonight. He began to be sorry he had taken a night job. How many more police cars would he meet? How many more times would he be questioned and bullied and shaken? This was worse than trudging through the jungle! He broke into a trot.

Now he was nearing the place where the gas was rationed out to those whom the government decided were justified in driving cars. It was a street lined with big houses, important-looking places, many of which bore a name-plate on the iron gates at the front of the driveways. The name-plates had the names of South Africa, Tanzania and Ghana on them. Jonah would not have guessed that they were embassy houses. Nor would he have understood what an embassy was.

He had only half a block to go now. He slowed to a quick walk. Suddenly, out of the driveway of one of the big houses, a bulky figure stepped into the moonlight, barring Jonah's way. It was Judas! His gold fillings were gleaming as he grinned evilly, triumphantly. "So! You thought you had escaped us by moving out of the Location. Ha!"

Jonah was now thoroughly frightened – and with good reason. He tried to dart past the outstretched arms, but Balatwa was too quick for him. The big man grabbed the youth and half-dragged, half-wrestled him into the darkness of the driveway. Jonah struggled desperately, his despairing cries getting louder. "Let me go! I will not do your evil work! I am staying with the Mfundisi! He knows——"

A savage swing of a blackjack to his head silenced Jonah! It didn't knock him out, but took the spark from his struggle.

"Give me a hand, Mbambo!" grunted Judas. Mbambo was the driver of the long, black sedan parked in the driveway.

The two struggled with Jonah, trying to force him into the car. Jonah's head was clearing now and he resumed his attempt to get away. He knew he stood no chance but put every ounce of strength into resisting. He somehow guessed that Mbambo was a government man – most likely from Zambia – and that Balatwa had taken refuge in the Zambian embassy, knowing that the police could not touch him there. Jonah's mind quickly finished the next part of the puzzle. This Mbambo would take him to Zambia – to the Lion! He would have no trouble crossing the border into Zambia. Although the two countries, Southern and Northern Rhodesia (now Zambia), were enemies since Ian Smith's independent move, there was still a pretense at diplomatic dealings. They were merely for convenience and to keep the wheels turning on the mines and railways.

Balatwa let go of Jonah with one arm – the one with the blackjack. Jonah did not see the long arm raise and come down with force. He felt it hit for a brief instant, then blackness of feeling nothing.

He was tied and rudely thrown into the back seat. Balatwa said a few words to the driver, and the car moved off. Then Judas disappeared into the Embassy. He had done his job; it was to get Jonah well on his way to Zambia. He now had to make his way back to South Africa – if he could!

Piercing the blackness of his sleep, Jonah gradually became aware of sounds and movement. It was all like a dream, the bumping, the swerving, when his body rolled from one side to the other. The car honked once or twice. One time it swerved violently, as though dodging some obstacle, and Jonah was thrown against the door.

The bump shook away some of the mist from his brain. He began to think, and at once every nerve became alert. His head throbbed as feeling came back slowly.

They're taking me to Zambia! he reasoned when the fog was gone from his brain. At one time he had thought it was inevitable; he had to go. Nothing could prevent it. And he did not much care. He was like that twig floating on a swift stream, rushing toward the cataract. Much had happened since that similar trip to the Rhodesian border, when Tarzan and Baswana had started him on his journey. Then, he was what the White Man calls a "fatalist." It was no use struggling against the goal that Fate had marked out for you. Like that twig, whirled along by the strong force of the water, you couldn't do a thing. To resist meant to wear out your strength and to make you feel more helpless and hopeless. In those days he knew he was a plaything in the hands of evil men. What could his puny strength do against so much Bad Medicine?

As the car roared along Jonah's mind lit up with the thought that he was now different! So many things had happened to make him realize that the Great- Great does take an interest in the lowliest and least of His creation – *even me, Jonah, the Hyena,* he thought. Right from the start! There was Miriam! His heart warmed as he recalled her soft voice as she spoke to him, lying despairing in the old car in the dark garage, shivering with the cold and fright and hunger. Just a few words she had spoken – words that could have been rough and impatient, showing her contempt of this unknown criminal. But she had spoken kindly to him; she had promised to help him – to speak of him to his only friends – Moses, the lawyer, and Gideon, the minister.

The car paused in its mad rush, turned to the left, with a grinding of gears, and resumed its mad rush. Jonah was alert; thinking feverishly. *How can I escape? How can I escape?* He knew now he could never go to Zambia. That was the worst possible thing that could happen to him. His friends would never be able to reach him there. Both South Africa and Rhodesia were poison to the Zambians. The two countries represented the worst to the African – White Supremacy! Jonah knew with a certainty what he had never before experienced, that his only hope lay in returning to South Africa with his only human hope, Mr. Pendelton!

He wrestled with the rope that tied his hands behind him, but it would not yield. The tight cords were well tied and only burned his wrists as he struggled. He must escape! *"In Thee do I hope . . ."* he prayed wistfully. Was there hope? Would he stand the slightest chance of getting out of the clutches of this one called Mbambo? He was a different person from Balatwa. Even with the slight glimpse he had gotten of him in the struggle in the dark, Jonah knew he was a smoother character. He was a well-dressed, and probably well-educated, diplomat. Yet the fact that he had helped to subdue Jonah and allowed the violence without a protest, showed he was ruthless.

Jonah's mind flashed back to the evidences of divine help all along the way – his friends of the road, the truck-drivers; the kindness of the girl of the beer-hall; the Websters. And that Lenten service, when he had been so impressed by Mr. Webster's description of the sufferings of the Saviour of the world. And the commitment he had made in that service. Yes, he was different! It hadn't happened all of a sudden; it had been gradual. But this Jonah, lying on the floor of a limousine, was a vastly different Jonah from the shivering escapee sitting in the station wagon, rushing toward a fate he dreaded, with every man's hand against him.

Once across that border into hostile Zambia, Mr. Pendelton's influence could not help him. All the skill of Moses Mapomulo could not reach him; all the love of Reverend Mukalo – and Mfundisi Beckwith – would be lost. Jonah's groping fingers touched a bracket on the floor of the car. Perhaps he could use it to fray the ropes. He wriggled his body until he felt the bonds were up against the bracket, and he prayed there might be same rough spot, some slight point that would act as a saw. He worked frantically, gritting his teeth against the pain of the tight ropes cutting into his wrists, and the rough scraping of his skin against the bracket. He gritted his teeth as the skin was pinched and twisted.

How far was it to the border? Somehow, he thought it was a good way. He had learned that the two cities, Bulawayo and Salisbury, were somewhere near the middle of the nation. But the car was a good, fast one. It would not take long to get to the frontier, speeding along the paved highways with no other traffic, at that time of night.

Jonah was sweating now, his breath coming in quick gasps. Luckily the noise of the car prevented Mbambo from hearing him. With a final, painful effort Jonah strained at the cords.

The rope gave! Jonah lay, sweating and shaking. If Mbambo caught on he would find Jonah an easy mark to tie up again; the youth felt so weak.

But Mbambo drove on. He had one thought in his mind – to get to Lusaka, and deliver this ignorant fugitive of a Zulu to Simba! Like many diplomats, Mbambo was in the spy game. He knew of Kwanda's work, and had had many a talk with Balatwa about the all-Black Continent which he knew would one day come about. He was confident that, with all the independent nations of Africa uniting, and the placing of Black Men in positions of power and authority, it would have to take place. It was only a question of time. As to this Jonah, this escapee Judas had called "The Hyena," it was his business to get him across the border and hand him over. What became of him after that, he couldn't care less!

The first time we stop! thought Jonah. He must stop for gas or food somewhere along the way. Jonah had seen a map of Rhodesia in the office of the petrol storage place. He had studied it to see what route he could follow to get to the border. He had noticed the names of places along the thin red line that meant a road – a highway. There was Banket, then Sinoia. After that, the road ran up to the great Kariba Dam, with its huge, man-made lake, and the great river Zambezi. That was the border. Once across the Zambezi, he was lost. Perhaps forever. Kwanda had not discussed his return. It was one thing to get over a border, but quite another to get back again. Especially with the tension rising daily between North and South Rhodesia!

The car was slowing! Was it a simple slowdown for a turn? Or a real stop? Jonah's heart was pounding now! He had made up his mind what to do. *The moment the car stops, I will open the door and dash off*. What he would do after that didn't matter. He would be on his own. He did not think Mbambo would have a weapon; even if he had, would he use it? Jonah did not waste any more time thinking.

He did not wait for the car to stop. Crouching between the back and front seats, so Mbambo would not know his captive had broken free from the bonds, he waited his chance. Mbambo saw him just as he reached for the door handle. The car was still moving. The driver reached back his hand and grabbed Jonah's shoulder. The car swerved. Jonah put all his strength into his fist, striking the driver on the neck and freeing himself. The youth flung open the door and jumped. He fell, sprawling on his face and rolled several times to break the fall. Then he was up like a cat falling from a tree, looking to see where he could hide.

Yes, it was a small town. White-washed buildings were scattered widely. Ahead – about fifty meters – was a service station, lit up. Evidently Mbambo was making for that!

The car had stopped. Mbambo was shouting; he was tumbling out of the car. Men from the service station were looking, wondering whether to remain where they were or take part in the chase. Jonah had seen enough; he ran back down the highway, hoping the darkness would swallow him up before his pursuers caught up with him. No shots rang out! For that he was grateful. He heard footsteps pounding behind him. He could only make out one pair, probably Mbambo's. Jonah was making for a patch of trees he could see dimly ahead. The moon was partly hidden by clouds; he wished it were pitch dark. The footsteps behind him grew fainter. Mbambo could not keep Jonah's pace. He reached the trees and dodged between them. He was safe, for the moment. He stopped, gasping for breath, and leaned up against one of the blue gums. He listened. He could hear no noises but knew Mbambo would not give up so easily. He would have to give an account to his leaders – to say nothing of Balatwa. No, Jonah knew he could not stay there long. What would Mbambo do? He tried to think. He would likely turn his car around and drive slowly along the highway for a distance, looking for the fugitive. Then he would return to the town and send a wire or a phone message through, one to Balatwa and another to the Lion, warning them that the prisoner had escaped. Would he ever be free from pursuit? Was he always doomed to forever run, run, run? An hour or two before this he had felt so safe. Friends were helping him; he had a nice place to stay. Then this – far out in the wilderness, a more remote desolation than the land through which he had come a few days previous.

Again Jonah did a strange thing, for an escaping convict. He knelt among those eucalyptus trees and again communed with Nkulunkulu – the Great-Great – and His Son, *Ujesu Kristu.*

Strengthened, he rose to his feet; he knew just what he would do. Walk south, off the highway, until the morning, then hitch a ride again. He knew what would happen . . . just as God had sent help before, in the form of trucks and happy truck-drivers, He would do it again.

He heard the sound of a car. Could it be Mbambo, coming back as he had expected him to? Would he not search this very clump of trees? Jonah saw the black car – he recognized it by its long, low shape. Sure enough, it stopped just opposite to where he stood. Quick as his thoughts, Jonah looked for a tree to climb. The blue gums are bare and smooth; the bark peels off in paper-like flakes that hang down like wallpaper peeling off a wall. He must shin up the tree! It was not easy but when a man is desperate he can do such things. Jonah put his arms and legs around the smooth trunk and inched his way up. He slipped back slightly, so he gripped the trunk even more tightly. He could hear voices. Evidently Mbambo had got someone to help him search, likely one of the men from the service station. Jonah was sweating and his hands slipped, the bark digging into his already cut wrists, but up he went, steadily. Now he could see a limb jutting out to the right. He must reach it before they came near. He reached up, he could almost touch it, but it was still out of reach. Another tremendous effort. He almost lost his balance but caught the limb. Painfully, he pulled himself up and swung one leg over, then the other. More limbs were easy to reach, like the rungs of a ladder. Up he went. Now he was completely out of sight of those below.

Jonah looked down. Two dark figures were coming. A light went before them, searching the ground and flashing among the trees. Jonah shrank back against the huge trunk of the tree. He kept as still as a *gazelle* freezing at the sight of its enemies.

"I saw him come in here!" It was Mbambo's smooth, cultured voice, but just now it had an angry edge to it.

"Maybe long way away now, *Bwana!*" The garage man did not seem happy to be searching in the jungle at midnight. Africans do not like the nighttime. One reason is that is when the evil spirits are abroad. And somehow those who have mastered their fears find them rushing back into their minds at night.

"Just look around for a minute!" Mbambo's words were sharp. He was a diplomat, used to being obeyed.

The two flashed their lights around for a few more feet then came back. The man was fearful and expressed it in his grumbling; Mbambo was silent. They returned to the car; it moved on, still heading south. Jonah decided to stay where he was until he saw it returning. He had found a place in the tree where the dividing branches made a support for his back as he sat in the crotch. Where could he be safer? He leaned against the limbs, exhausted. Finally he allowed himself the luxury of closing his eyes and in a moment was asleep.

15

THE SHRILL CRIES of a bird awoke him. The sky was brightening; it was nearing dawn. Jonah looked about him in amazement. When he saw the ground far below him, he nearly fell off his perch! He had actually slept, like a bird on a roost, for three or four hours! Instinctively, he had kept a tight hold on one of the many branches that jutted out all around him, and only this, and the shape of the crotch, had kept him from falling. He felt stiff and sore and it was a painful climb down the tree. His wrists were beginning to heal but still smarted. When he saw the length of the smooth, bare trunk up which he had climbed he could not understand how he had done it.

The bird was still keeping up a sharp cry. It seemed to want to attract Jonah's attention, for it flew back and forth, then settled on a twig near where he stood.

"Why, it's the honey bird!" His face lit up. This was another way the Great-Great was helping him. Jonah had followed the "honey-guide" in his own Zululand. This amazing little creature usually co-operates with the badger to rob the wild bees' nest. The badger (or *ratel,* as it is called in Africa) is very fond of honey and has a hide like well-tanned leather which the bees cannot penetrate. But when no *ratel* comes in answer to his chirp, the honey bird fearlessly seeks the help of man. His voice sounded like the word "quick! quick!" and Jonah responded gladly. He was glad to see the little thing fly south. "That's the way I'm going, my friend," he laughed.

There was nothing but bush and veld ahead. He followed the bird as fast as his aching limbs would let him, and it flew from bush to bush, impatiently uttering its "Quick! Quick!"

As the bird drew nearer to the site of the honey it became more excited and flew jabbering, from the man to bushes and back to man again. It stopped above a great fallen mahogany tree that had lain on the jungle floor so long its massive trunk was rotting. Jonah saw a few bees coming from a spot near the end of the trunk. How would he get the honey now that he and his bird-friend had found it? "Only one way, my honey bird," he said aloud. "Smoke! And you, you crafty bird! You know man has the materials to make smoke!"

Jonah looked around for some dry stuff to burn. Luckily it had not rained and he found some dry grass. It was still damp enough from the dew to smoke well. He pulled a book of matches from his shirt pocket and lit the materials, fanning the smoke into the hollow log.

Pulling his hat as low over his head as he could and turning up his coat collar, Jonah tackled the hazardous job of getting the honey as he had done it in his home country. He got a few stings, but what is that compared to the tangy, wild taste of honey in the comb? The bird did not let him forget its share. It fluttered about, shrilling its urgent call, and he threw it a generous chunk of honeycomb. "You can have the young bees, too," he laughed. "I don't want them!"

Nothing had ever tasted so good. Jonah was hungry. He saw no prospect of getting food for a long time and this heaven-sent gift was grand. Far more delicious than the honey you buy in the stores, Jonah thought, as he sat on a rock and ate to his stomach's content.

"Good-by, little bird! You probably saved my life!" Jonah took off his hat and bowed to his friend, busy gobbling up the grubs. Then he strode off, keeping the sun on his left hand. He did not want to go too near the highway until he was sure he had shaken his pursuers, although he figured that Mbambo was well on his way to Lusaka by this time. Still, he knew he was still a fugitive. Best to keep out of sight until I am sure, he mused.

Jonah thought he must have lain unconscious in the car for at least one hour, perhaps two. That meant that Mbambo's car had traveled, perhaps 60 to 100 miles. Jonah trudged steadily onward, keeping a wary eye out for animal life. He was in a district that abounded in game of all kinds.

He walked the jungle and veld for six hours, avoiding the highway. But when the height of the sun told him it was around noon, he was tired and hungry enough to want to seek not only a ride but a meal.

Cautiously Jonah made his way through the trees and bush until he saw those sure-fire signs of civilization, telegraph poles. Wherever the White Man goes he must have his wires. And no matter how many times Africans climb those poles and cut the copper wires – to sell them for a few shillings on the black market – the White Man patiently drives out in his repair truck and replaces them. Jonah thought how often he had accompanied his *tsotsi* "friends" on some of these wire-stealing forays. They knew of a junk dealer in a back street who would take all the copper wire you could bring him! Jonah felt good to realize that those days of wildness and wrong-doing were gone forever. His wanderings in the wilderness had done one good thing for him – they had cured him of his desire to be dishonest. He longed for a chance of going to those same *tsotsis* and telling them of his change of heart.

Jonah crouched among some high grass. He did not want to be seen by drivers of White Man's cars, as several roared along the highway, going either north or south. But after an hour he heard the distant, well-known rumble of a big vehicle. Jonah peered out from his hiding place. Yes, it was a truck, and two black faces showed through the windshield. Jonah stepped out and displayed the sign of the uplifted thumb. The truck's brakes squealed and it rumbled to a halt. The driver's face seemed one wide grin, with white teeth gleaming in the sunlight. Jonah clambered aboard, while the driver introduced himself. "I am Michael. Who be you?"

The truck moved off as Jonah answered, "My name is . . . Joseph."

Michael reached into the back of the truck and brought out a brown paper packet. Opened, it revealed a man-sized beef sandwich. "You look hungry!" Eat up," he commanded. "I'll get another at the petrol stop."

Gratefully Jonah took the sandwich and swallowed a mouthful hastily. *It's true what Mfundisi Mukalo said,* he thought, *the Curse would disappear when I let God into my heart. I've had so many good things happen to me. I'm not afraid of the Bad Medicine any more! Look at the way help has come along – just when I needed it most.*

Michael honked furiously and swerved to avoid running down a group of *spring-bok* that leaped gracefully across the road. "Feel better, my friend?"

"Much better. Thank you. Say . . . how far to Salisbury?"

"Not far . . . maybe an hour."

The truck rushed on. Jonah felt happier than he had since his last escapade. This Michael was like his namesake . . . an angel. Of all the men in Africa he'd rather have seen at the moment, he didn't know who it would be . . unless his other truck driving friends.

God did hear prayers! He was trying to digest this amazing thought. *The Great-Great, He who had the whole universe to bother about, seems to know just what I am thinking, even away out in the wilderness,* thought Jonah. *And it seems as though He wants us to believe that. If we do, He helps us. Faith makes all the difference.*

Jonah vaguely recalled the Great-Great's Word said something like "without faith it is impossible to please God." His heart was full of hope. Even if he had to go back to Johannesburg and take his punishment, he knew everything would work out right. Surely the black cloud of the Curse had been dissipated and the sun was able to shine through.

A half an hour more, and the outlying buildings of Salisbury came into view. "You want a ride to the Union?"

"Thank you, no!" replied Jonah.

"Well, I'm making for the tobacco warehouse," said Michael. "Could I let you off there, or somewhere else?"

"That'll be fine," said Jonah. "It isn't far from the manse. I think I'll find my friends there!" His heart beat high, and his eyes lit up as he spoke.

"Here we are!" The African drew his truck up by the side of a platform flanking a huge barn of a place. The smell of tobacco gushed out from the vast doors. The two alighted and stood.

Michael held out a big paw. "Well, see you again sometime, maybe," he laughed.

Jonah felt a pang as he pictured where he might see him. He shook hands heartily. "Thank you for the food and the ride." Again a firm clasp and Jonah turned away. Soon he was striding along Jameson Street, elated at the thought of meeting his friends again.

He did not go up the front steps and ring the bell. Only the White *Baases* do that. Africans must "keep their places." Not that the ministers would have noticed it, but Jonah had centuries of humility bred in to him. He went around to the back door and stood there, hoping some one would see him and he would be saved from having to knock or ring. He could hear Mrs. Webster moving about, humming a little tune. After a time she caught sight of him.

"Why didn't you knock, Jonah?" she said. "And where have you been? You look as though you've been through the mill since we saw you last night!"

She went into the front room, and called out, "The wanderer has returned! Come through, Jonah!"

Jonah came timidly into the kitchen and then the lounge. Mr. Webster and Mr. Pendelton were on their feet, hands outstretched.

Jonah stepped forward, and greeted them.

"Well, well," said the visitor. "You have gone through much tribulation since we last met – in the courtroom! Mr. Webster has been telling me all about it! But I believe you're a better man today because of all your troubles! Oh . . . I say! Those wrists . . . can we get something for them?"

Jonah tried to speak, but the words would not come. He could only stare and grin. He wanted so much to tell Mr. Pendelton how he appreciated all he had done for him, but the words stuck in his throat. Then he managed, "Thank you! I am all right. My arms are all right, too."

"Sit down! Sit down! You must be tired! Mother, is the tea still hot? Bring Jonah a cup!" But Mrs. Webster was already coming forward with the refreshment, and Jonah was grateful this time for the fragrant English beverage and the biscuits.

In between sips, he told them of his experience. They were shocked. Their looks grew even more serious when he mentioned the violence that had been shown the night before. "So the diplomats are now getting into it," murmured Mr. Webster. "I've often seen that Mbambo – a smooth customer – but I never suspected he would get mixed up with a chap like Judas Balatwa!" He shook his head. "But you got away! Zambia is a closed door to most folk these days. Oh, I dare say I might have got through on a pretext of visiting one of my missions up at Mazabuka, but if they'd caught me helping a fugitive, one of their agents——" He paused.

Mr. Pendelton set down his cup and bent towards Jonah. "I don't suppose you've heard the good news?" He sat back. "We've found the murder weapon!"

Jonah's heart began beating like a jungle drum. His eyes widened and a great wave of joy swept over him. "Found – found! How – who——!" He was stammering in his confusion.

"Your good friend, Mapomulo, went to Tarzan's room. You knew he and your fat friend, Kwanda, have been arrested? Yes . . .

well, after a lot of false starts he found where Tarzan had hidden the gun!"

His face grew grave. "Of course the battle's not won yet, by a long chalk! You'll have to stand trial – on the original charge, of course——"

Jonah's face fell. "Must I still face——?"

Mr. Pendelton help up his hand. "Now, don't start getting discouraged. You've a lot in your favor. Moses is preparing his case with the skill and thoroughness for which he is noted. Mr. Mukalo is also working on your behalf, and I'll do my best to see that old prejudices do not carry too much weight!"

Mr. Webster rose. "If you've finished your tea, Jonah, I think you'd better come with me to the police station and tell them what Balatwa and Mbambo did. We won't need to say anything about your past. All they need to know is that you were a – well, valued employee of the Petrol Storage center, and that you were on your way to work and were set upon by two men, one of whom you recognized, and simply bundled into a car. Kidnapped, in short! That's a vile offense in any country!"

"Do you think it's wise to mention Mbambo?" put in Mrs. Webster. "Jonah didn't know him, and we can't prove he was involved." Mr. Webster sat down.

The two ministers sat thoughtful for a moment. At last Pendelton said: "I think your wife has something there, Sam! Mbambo will get all that's coming to him one of these days! He's probably trembling in his shoes right now, wondering if Jonah will report him – or, at least, the black, shiny car that was parked in the Zambian embassy driveway!"

"But you're safe in reporting Balatwa. He's an alien, and an undesirable character. Still, I wonder if he hasn't left town already? Jonah said he mentioned returning to the Rand. Said he had more important work to do there, or else he would have gone on to Zambia!" put in Mrs. Webster.

Jonah shifted uncomfortably. "Sir, if you don't mind——"

"Go on, my boy! Get it off your chest!"

"Well, I'd rather you didn't mention either Balatwa or Mbambo to the police. I'd much rather return to Johannesburg with you than to have them take me! I think they will hold me once I am found. Wouldn't they have a description of me? The Rand Police knew I had crossed the border."

Mr. Webster laughed. "Well, for once I've been outwitted by

my wife and a friend and Jonah, here. Still, thinking it over, I guess you're all in the clear! The less we say about Jonah the better." He turned to Pendelton. "You won't be going back until the day after Easter Monday, I suppose? And if the police here get hold of Jonah they'll wire right away to the Rand, and it's good-by Jonah!"

"What–what about my job?" asked Jonah. "I ought to go and apologize for not showing up last night. But I won't say what happened."

"You could say you overslept!" chuckled Webster.

"Just say there were circumstances over which you had no control!" put in Pendelton. "No! Sam here'll go with you, and say you were not well. That's true enough. Just when you should have begun your work, you were certainly not well!"

Jonah and Mr. Webster arose and set off for the center. As they walked along Mr. Webster asked Jonah if he intended working until he left town.

"I might as well," said Jonah. "They'll likely want me to work through Good Friday and Saturday. Trucks are pouring in all the time. But I don't want to miss the sunrise service Sunday, or the other services of the day."

The manager of the storage depot glared at Jonah when they entered the office. "Where were you last night? Oh, excuse me, sir! You're with him, are you?" His politeness seemed rather forced.

Mr. Webster took no notice. He was used to that treatment. Anyone who champions the cause of the Negro must expect it. "I just came along with the lad. He wants to explain where he was last night. I assure you he would have been here. In fact, he was on his way, when——"

"Oh, that's all right! Is he prepared to work all the harder tonight? And, of course, there's no let up for Easter. No time for sentiment here, y'know!"

"I'd like Sunday off, sir," put in Jonah.

The man looked from Jonah to the minister. "Well, I suppose if you must you must. Church, I suppose?"

"Might do you good, too," smiled Mr. Webster. "Well, thanks for accepting the lad's explanation. Come on Jonah!"

As the two walked back to the manse the pastor said, "There's just one thing worrying me, Jonah. How's Mr. Pendelton going to get you back over the border? Your passport, by what you've told me, is false – made out to – who was it? Joseph somebody? Yes, and I don't think Pendelton would like you to be sailing under false colors, to speak. Moreover, I don't think he'd agree to any tricky work – like your hiding in the back seat, or in the trunk."

He mentioned the matter to the visiting parson when they were seated again in the front room, after supper and Jonah had gone to his own room.

The two sat thinking for some time. At last Pendelton said, "The only thing to do is simply to say he's the fugitive they've been seeking, and I'm taking him back to custody – and to his lawyer. It's an awkward situation, whichever way you look at it."

"I've got another idea," said Webster. "Let him go as Joseph Panzani. And you can safely say he's a student, bound for Fort Hare College. The lad's keen on getting an education. He had a long talk with David Ubangi, a student at the University here, and he told me Jonah would give anything to enter Fort Hare. We know he won't get into the college there just yet awhile, but he's 'bound' for the place. And I'll do all I can to help the boy get his wish!"

Mr. Pendelton looked serious. "I don't like anything savoring of deceit, but I also know what might happen if we are perfectly straightforward and lay all our cards on the table!" He gave his colleague a meaningful look.

"I can just see them dragging him out of your car, badgering and bullying him, shipping him to Jo'burg, and keeping him in chains until the trial!"

"That's just what I'm afraid of. You should have seen Jonah when I first saw him – in the court-room. He was absolutely cowed! A wreck of a man. Now he's been shown a bit of kindness, and has blossomed out like a flower in the desert! We don't want him to be kicked back into the slough of despond again. It'll make a lot of difference at the trial if he appears as a desperate-looking *tsotsi* or as a future student. I think we'll have to get him some clothes while he's here. He only has what he stands up in!"

"I thoroughly agree!"

16

TO JONAH, THAT EASTER WEEKEND was like a bright star in a night sky. He worked part of Good Friday to make up for his lost night but was able to take in the three-hour morning service. He did not have to go in to work until Saturday night and so was able to accompany Mr. Webster to a native clothier and get fitted up with a decent suit. Then, out of the "missionary barrel" Mrs. Webster gave him shirts, ties and shoes. For the Sunday services he looked "like a student," Mrs. Webster said. Jonah felt more self-respect than he had ever experienced. He *felt* like a student, and the others said he looked like one. He was glad to sit with David in the church.

His infant faith was strengthened as the events of the Calvary and Easter story were underlined by Bible reading, singing and talk. He felt the last remaining shadows of the Curse sink away as he realized how sane and wholesome were the teachings of Christianity.

Jonah was a little nervous as he went to work each night. He looked long and carefully at each black patch of shadow and was prepared to run if he saw anything suspicious. But he never saw the black, shiny car in the driveway again. He had heard rumors that the Embassy might pull out – the tension between the two countries was too much; perhaps that was why he saw no signs of life about the place over that Easter weekend.

Mr. Webster had spoken to David about the plan to get Jonah across the border into the Union as a student "bound for Fort Hare." David thought of another idea. "Why not ask Professor Waterson to write a letter for him? He could honestly say Jonah was going into the Union to make inquiries as to the possibility of entering Fort Hare. Jonah will certainly have to do that – not now, of course, but eventually!"

Professor Waterson was introduced to Jonah. He put many questions to the youth; asked him if he was really interested in getting more of an education. Did he want to go to Fort Hare when his time of trouble was over? Jonah was very sure. His eyes shone at the thought of mingling with men like David Ubangi and going about the grounds of the college with an armful of books and a pencil stuck behind his ear.

"You realize it means hard work, much study?" said the professor.

"I'm prepared to work hard," said Jonah, simply.

The professor took a sheet of college note paper and penned his letter. "I hope your dreams come true, my son," he said, as he handed Jonah the letter. Jonah put it carefully in the inside pocket of his new suit. His eyes were bright with hope. *How strange,* he thought, *that the thing we dread – the future that looks so black and hopeless to us – often turns out better than the time that went be-*

fore it! How I hated the plan Kwanda had made for my life! And it was a devilish plan. But God swept this plan aside like the housewife sweeps the cobwebs from the window. And He made another plan. Just like Joseph of the Bible when his brothers sold him into slavery, thinking that was the end of him when it was only the gateway to a wonderful career. They meant evil, but God turned it to good. Just as He had "turned the Curse into a blessing."

It was hard for Jonah to say good-by to the Websters. He stood there, in his new clothes, holding his suitcase (the first one he had owned) and his words would not come easily. His face seemed to be flushed behind the bronze and he found it hard to stand still.

"Mfundisi," he said at last, in a sudden way, "I don't know how to thank you . . ."

Mrs. Webster shook his hand. "You can show your gratitude, Jonah, by making good at school. Oh, I know you'll get over this – this problem of yours. It may be hard for a time, but keep believing – the sun will shine. Then, off to college! We're going to help, and I'm sure your Jo'burg friends'll chip in. And you'll have to find some kind of job, even while you're at college, to help meet your expenses. But we'll be pulling for you – and praying! So buck up!"

Mr. Webster lifted his suitcase into the back of the car. "Got that letter safe, my boy? Don't lose it! And stick to your 'Joseph' name until you're away from the danger zone. In fact, I think you'd better hang on to that name altogether! Joseph was a successful character. Jonah was a chap who ran away from duty, then, when he had preached his warning message, and when God didn't destroy the city, he sulked! Yes . . . I think you'd better change your name to Joseph!"

All four laughed. It was Tuesday morning. "Lovely day for traveling," said Mr. Webster. "Wish I were coming with you! Give our regards to the folk down there who know us! Good-by!"

The motor started, the car drove out of the driveway and turned on to the road. Jonah looked back. The Mfundisi and his good lady stood in the garden, waving and smiling. Jonah's throat seemed to tighten. It was hard to keep having to say good-by to friends – people whom perhaps he would never see again! Yet it seemed to be the regular thing all through life. He sat staring straight ahead, feeling a little melancholy at first. Then the sunlight streamed into his heart again. It was hard to feel glum on that lovely day.

"Good thing we started early," said Mr. Pendelton. "With God's good blessing we should be at the Beit Bridge by noon!"

There were very few people around at that early hour. A few Africans – some on bicycles, some on foot – were on their way to work. Shutters were being taken down from the store fronts. Milk boys were out, their white bottles rattling in the carriers of their bikes. But as always, the police vans moved silently but surely around the streets, a sign of the power of the White Man. Just the sight of those sleek vehicles, with their helmeted occupants, brought home to the Africans the thought of guns, tanks, planes, bombs – all the marks of might. Jonah's mind was full of these things as the car moved quickly through the city toward the open highway.

They passed through the Location. Jonah turned his head as the car moved along. It would likely be his last glimpse of the place that had been his home for a few days. He thought of Demas and Stephen who had befriended him once again in that place. His smile faded as he caught a glimpse of the door to his room and recalled the horrible feelings that went through him when, first, he saw Judas Balatwa, with his metal teeth and his fat cigar, and, second, when he discovered the *kalalozi* gun. He shivered even though the day was warm. Well, thank God that was all over now.

The car sped on. Mr. Pendelton concentrated on his driving. He was anxious to get on as far as he could; it was a long journey and he was keen to get the trip over in daylight. It is not good for the White Man to travel too much at night in these days. Many frightful "accidents" have happened to cars and their riders, on not only lonely roads, but busy highways that are not so busy in the dead of night!

Jonah brightened as he realized that every turn of the wheel brought him nearer to Miriam! Then he worried a little. Where was she? Her *baas* had been arrested; what had become of her? Then his jaw set. He would find her! Wherever she had gone in the whole of the vast city of Goldie he would find her. Perhaps they could go to college together. She must get an education, too. It would not do for him to learn so much more than his wife. He smiled at the daring nature of the thought which struck him.

The car was eating up the miles now. A few other cars and a few trucks were also out, some going south, some north. The vast veld stretched before them and all around them, a faint mist rising from its low-lying surfaces. Animal life is never absent in the country parts of Africa. Those night-prowlers – the lion, the leopard, the hyena, the cheetah, the jackal and the fox—were loping wearily back to their dens, ready for an all-day sleep. The grass-eaters were taking over. Different kinds of graceful deer were skipping happily toward the water-holes. How much happier they seem than the meat-eaters, thought Jonah. Herds of *wildebeeste (gnus)* galloped in the distance, raising a cloud of dust. The small heads of giraffe could be seen poking innocently above the tallest trees. It was always a heartening sight to Jonah. The wildlife in his own land had been driven north by the coming of man, but up here it was still much as nature had intended it to be.

About ten a.m. the minister slowed up and drove over to a sturdy wayside table, set under wild fig-trees with glossy leaves.

"Let's stretch our legs a bit, Jonah," he said. He went to the trunk, lifted the lid, and took out a basket which he set on the table. Jonah was standing, sniffing in the fragrant air of the open veld with its tang of blossoms.

"Come and sit down, Jonah! Mrs. Webster has thoughtfully provided a little refreshment."

The coffee, fresh and hot from the thermos, tasted like nectar, and the sandwiches and chicken-legs tasted better than usual with the added sauce of the pure air. They ate contentedly, chatting about the journey and what might happen at the Limpopo.

"Don't say any more than you have to, Jonah," advised Mr. Pendelton. "You were at the Easter services; I'll just say you found I was returning to the Rand, and got a ride with me. Then all you have to do is to pull out Professor Waterson's letter——"

"Quiet! Do not move!"

Jonah's voice cut in, his tone so hard, so menacing that Mr. Pendelton hardly recognized it. His face showed his astonishment and indignation. What was Jonah saying? "Don't move an inch, Mfundisi! You'll startle it and it'll strike. When you're under control, move as slowly as the turtle."

The minister's scalp crept. *What on earth was it?* He kept perfectly still, then slowly, although his whole body tingled and he longed to dash away, he pulled himself off the picnic-style bench and deliberately fell over backward. He was up in a moment, rolling over and over to get away from whatever danger he knew Jonah had warned him against. Meanwhile Jonah seized a hefty stick from the ground and was striking at a bright green hose hanging from the tree.

Mr. Pendelton's face went the color of paper. "Good heavens – a *mamba!*" Africa's most deadly snake. It loves to hang down from a tree and strike at the unwary man or animal that passes underneath.

With the first blow the snake had lost its hold and fallen on to the table. In the same movement it slid off the table. Jonah instantly recoiled as if his life depended on it – and it did – as the snake unleashed itself like an arrow at Jonah's leg. The fangs missed their target by a scant inch or two. Then the green serpent began to move away like quicksilver. Jonah shouted, his skin crawling, and brought the club down with all his fury on the snake. The wiry reptile shook off the blow, turned and came at its attacker again with its fangs showing. This time Jonah caught it on the head, splattering it in the dry dust. In a frenzy the youth continued beating at the green snake until it was evident the deadly reptile was itself dead. Jonah fell to the bench, panting for breath, shaking and repulsed by it all.

Mr. Pendelton was hastily throwing the thermos and scraps into the basket.

"Let's get out of here! Ugh! I go creepy all over when I think of that thing dangling above my head!" They both shivered again. "If you hadn't spoken when you did——" He mopped his forehead and, picking up the basket, walked to the car, placing what was left of the lunch in the trunk and banging down the lid.

When Jonah was seated beside him in the front seat he squeezed the youth's arm. "I'll never forget this, my boy!" he said quietly.

On they went, talking for the most part about the events of the last few minutes. "You can't be too careful in this land," said the minister at last, summing up his thoughts. "I could tell you some stories – well, you could tell me far more, I suppose, having lived in the wilds of Zululand. But one grows careless, and forgets to knock out his shoes in the morning, or picks up a tea-towel without shaking it, or sits down on a picnic bench without looking up into the trees to see if there are any uninvited guests to lunch!" He laughed. "Still, it's a grand country! I wouldn't live in any other."

"Nor I!" said Jonah. Both laughed.

They grew silent as the steel girders of the Beit Bridge showed in the distance. One little mistake, one little slip and Jonah would be grabbed, handcuffed, thrown into a room, and locked up to await the inevitable police van from the Rand.

"One good thing," said the pastor. "You look a lot different from the scarecrow you must have been when you escaped from the police – excuse me for that name! But I can imagine how you looked! Pull that felt hat well down. Put on a bright smile. Remember, you're an intelligent student, not an escaped *tsotsi*. With that nice collar and tie and suit, you look enough like David Ubangi to be his brother!"

Other cars were lining up at the customs and immigration offices, and Mr. Pendelton slowed the car and glided up behind the last one. Jonah tried not to tremble but something of the old terrified feeling persisted. It was always present when the White Police were near. He felt the reassuring pressure of the minister's hand on his arm and set his lips firmly. He must play the part. It would be too bad not only for him but for the parson if it were discovered that he was an escaped convict! As the cars ahead slowly moved on and his car came abreast of the gate, he put on a smile, although his face felt stiff as he did so.

The man took Mr. Pendelton's passport. "Just been on a visit to Salisbury, right?" said the man. He did not smile. He had no use for ministers, especially those who rode with Black Men. Mr. Pendelton nodded.

The man's cold eyes focused on Jonah, and it was all he could do to keep that smile going. "And who's the . . . er . . . native beside you?" Jonah handed the man his passport. "Joseph Panzani." The man's brows drew together in concentration as he scanned its pages. Jonah could hear the beating of his heart.

"A prospective student, off to make inquiries for admission to Fort Hare – that's the college for African's, you know," said the minister.

"I know," grunted the official.

The parson nudged Jonah. The lad reached into his inner pocket and drew out the letter from the Professor. The man looked at it as though he were trying to decipher a Chinese puzzle. "H'm, guess it's all right," he said. "Have to be careful letting natives into our country these days."

Jonah's heart was pumping but he kept what he hoped was an intelligent expression on and stilled his shaking limbs.

"On you go!" The man handed back the passports and papers and motioned the car to move forward. Jonah hardly dared breathe. He held his breath until the car was fully a hundred meters down the highway. They were safely in the Union! It was a miracle! "Thank God that's over," said Mr. Pendelton. He drew out his handkerchief and dabbed his forehead. "I wouldn't like to go through that experience every day! I'd not be much of a spy, I'm afraid."

Jonah kept looking back. He almost expected to hear the all-too-familiar siren and see an ominous car speeding after them, but the highway was bare of official-looking cars. They were safe!

He was exhausted after his double ordeal of killing the snake and getting through the customs. His head sank forward and as the car rushed smoothly along the paved road, he slept. It was with a start of suprise that he heard his companion say, "Wake up, Jonah! Here we are!"

It was dark! He had been dozing for hours! Jonah got out of the car stiffly and took his suitcase out of the car. He stood awkwardly for a minute or two. Where would he go? Not to his *tsotsi* friends. He would sooner go back to prison. "What are you standing there for? Come in! I have a surprise for you, my boy! As for where you are to stay, for tonight, at any rate, you stay right here! Tomorrow, we'll have to see about taking you to the court. But don't worry! We'll have Moses and Gideon with us, quite a strong escort, eh? Come on in, I guess my wife will be glad to see us!"

Jonah followed him up the steps. Mixed feelings were running riot in his mind. It was wonderful to know he had good friends, those who would see him through his trouble, but it was awful to realize he had to go back to that cold, stony prison, with its maddening loneliness and callous, intimidating guards.

"Mabel, this is Jonah! Where are you?" Mrs. Pendelton came quickly through into the front room. "Welcome home, Michael!" A mysterious smile came to her face. "I think someone else will be glad to see you!"

Who could she mean? Jonah was puzzled.

"Bring in the tea, please!"

Jonah sat down on the chesterfield, as he heard the jingle of teacups. He looked up idly. Then an electric shock went through his whole being. He jumped up, his face flaming under his dark brown hue. "Miriam!"

Miriam carefully put down the tray. Jonah walked over to her and their eyes met. Jonah felt he never wanted to look away from them. It was a long, long look in which all that was ever written about love was expressed. There was no need for words. Their eyes told the story. Jonah felt as though a warm glow spread into every fiber of his being. He took her hands and held them. No embrace, and yet their hearts were wrapped in each other.

"The tea's getting cold, Miriam. I think we'd better serve it!" Mrs. Pendelton was smiling, but her words broke the spell. Jonah returned to his seat and sat down. He was like one in a trance.

Miriam! Here! It was another miracle! And there was no mistaking that long look and the shining eyes. Husband and wife smiled at each other. Mrs. Pendelton noticed the rapt look in Jonah's eyes. "Miriam gets off duty tonight – after supper. Why don't you take her somewhere? There's a fine Easter play on at Trinity. I think she'd like to go."

Miriam had gone out, quickly and lightly. Mr. and Mrs. Pendelton laughed at Jonah's stammered thanks and confusion.

"I'll ring up Moses and Gideon," said Mr. Pendelton, when they had finished their supper. "They expected me back some time today. You don't need to stay, Jonah. We'll decide what is the best procedure for tomorrow. They said they'd come over as soon as I rang up."

"Whatever you decide will be all right with me," said Jonah, gratefully. "It's wonderful to be able to have one night – free." His eyes welled with tears of emotion and excitement.

"We hope you'll have many nights free – some day!" said the minister, clapping the youth on the back. "And if our plans work out, it won't be too long!"

Jonah, at Mrs. Pendelton's suggestion, found Miriam in the kitchen after supper. He asked if he might help her. As they worked together – she washing, he wiping – he shyly asked her if he might take her to the play.

"Oh, I don't know! What will Mrs. Pendelton say?"

"She was the one who suggested it!"

Miriam's laugh was like a silver bell. Jonah recalled that he had never heard her laugh. It was a pleasant laugh and he thought he would be pleased about everything he learned about this girl. Jonah had known hardship and want. *If Heaven is better than this,* he mused, *it must be grand!* He felt as if the bells were ringing and all the birds singing as he polished the cups and saucers and plates with intensity.

"I'll think about it," said Miriam.

There was a question he had been longing to ask Miriam. At last he found the courage. "Did you get my letter?"

Miriam carefully placed the gold-flowered teapot on the shelf, hung up a tea towel, and looked at Jonah. Again their eyes met, and Jonah knew that she not only received the letter, but had found a response of mutual love in her heart. Miriam felt in her apron pocket, and pulled out the worn and folded paper. "You – you – actually *kept* it?" Jonah felt he must be dreaming.

"I knew you weren't guilty, even before Tarzan brought you to Kwanda's place," said Miriam. "I knew Tarzan was the only one who owned a gun. Ugh! He's a bad one, that!" Her eyes flashed. "When he told me you were in the car, and that he was helping you escape, I felt sorry for you. I had read in the papers about the murder and I never thought you did it."

"Then you *did* manage to see Mr. Mapomulo?"

The girl nodded. "Then, when Kwanda was arrested, I did not know what to do. But my good *baas,* Mr. Pendelton, came to show the new editor the place, and he asked me to come and work for him. Are you glad I came?"

Jonah's eyes met hers again. "Glad!" There was no need to say more. He was like one in a dream as he waited for Miriam to get ready to go to the play; like one walking on air as he led her down the street, and, as he sat beside her in the church, he wished he might never wake up.

His hand timidly and awkwardly found hers when the hall was darkened for some of the scenes. The warm pressure she gave him in return sent a tingling shock up his arm. Only the shadow of the trial looming in the background of his mind was able to mar the evening. But youth is hopeful. It does not think of the future.

As they strolled toward home they laughed and talked, walking hand in hand. This lovely girl was to him even more lovely than his dreams of her had been. She told him about herself – her home, her parents and family, her hopes. He in turn brought her up to date. The words which had been only in his mind, not shared with anyone, he now revealed to her.

"If I can get free," he began, "I want to go to school. I have changed my ways and given my heart to *Ujesu Kristu.*" And he told her about the wonderful radiance and vitality life now held for him. He carefully prepared the way for his final words by telling her about his hopes for college.

Shyly, hesitantly, he took her hands as they stopped under a jacaranda tree in the night air. "And . . . and I want to share my life with . . . with——"

He did not need to finish. Miriam clearly understood his proposal.

Her reply was wordless but affirmative. Her eyes were now very close to his, looking lovingly and tenderly into the deep brown eyes of the youth. She squeezed his hands to let him know that she loved him.

Jonah was floating, soaring, oblivious to anything except his love for Miriam and the promise of their lives together as one. Let tomorrow bring its terror, he had strength to sustain him in the love of Miriam. And anyone could face life with that!

They were at the home of the Pendeltons now. They walked in through the back door into the kitchen. Miriam broke the silent spell. "We'd better say goodnight here."

He stammered, "Miriam . . . I – I . . . ."

The small light from the hall radiated around her face, giving it an aura of beauty and loveliness Jonah would always treasure and remember. It was Miriam who spoke again. "We'd better say goodnight! Thank you for the lovely evening. I'll be praying for you when the trial begins. I won't ever forget you!" She stretched on her toes and kissed him on the forehead. Again Jonah felt that tingling sensation.

"It's been the best evening of my life," he said, and she knew he meant it. Miriam ran off to her room and Jonah walked into the front room to see Mr. Pendelton.

In an instant all the rosy mist of the last few hours was swept rudely aside. Mr. and Mrs. Pendelton, Moses Mapomulo and Gideon Mukalo were standing, their faces showing dismay. In the center of the room stood a man in the hated khaki that Jonah knew so well. Glittering things dangled from his hands, held out toward Jonah. The White Police had found out he was back in town!

For one wild moment Jonah thought of dashing out the back door. But he had had enough of running. *Now I will face up to trouble,* he thought. *God will see me through!* He walked forward, his face a shade paler than its usual bronze, and held out his hands.

"I don't think there's any need of the handcuffs," said the minister.

The policeman laughed. "Oh, no? These chaps are slippery customers! And we've had enough trouble over this one. Lucky for us that chap Balatwa wrote Kwanda in prison and told him this murderer was with you, sir." The inflection was sarcastic. He continued. "He wrote that you planned to bring this man back to the Rand with you! We got word too late to stop you at the border, but we knew where to find you."

"You know we were planning to turn him in tomorrow," said Mr. Pendelton, his voice shaking. "And you know we have evidence to prove that this man is not guilty!"

The man slipped the handcuffs on Jonah's still-sore wrists and clicked them tight. "We'll let the judge decide that," he said harshly. "Come on, you!"

Jonah was pushed toward the front door. *Why had I not noticed the police van parked across the street from the manse. In too much of a lovely dream to notice it, I suppose,* he thought miserably. For a moment he was tempted to despair. Would this be the end to all his prospects and plans?

Then he set his jaw. No! It must not! He had had a glimpse of what life could offer to a man who was determined to do right – even if he was a despised Negro. He would not let this setback dash his hopes.

Mr. Pendelton came out to the van. The policeman and his partner tried to keep him away but he would not be denied.

"We're going to the prosecuting attorney tomorrow, Jonah." He whispered, "So don't lose heart! Moses tells me they're not waiting till the autumn assizes, because of this new evidence. We're trying to get the trial brought forward as soon as possible. Don't forget! Prayer changes things! No matter how spiteful man is, he cannot stand against God! And we'll be praying, too!"

He pressed Jonah's hand and watched the van drive away. When he turned, Miriam stood there, her eyes shining with tears, her handkerchief pressed to her lips.

"What–what–has happened, Mfundisi?" she gasped.

"Don't be afraid, Miriam! This won't make any difference in the long run. It only means Jonah will spend the night in a cold cell instead of in a nice bed!"

He put his arm around the girl's shoulders and led her back into the house.

"Well, this is a new development," said the minister, as the two Africans and Mrs. Pendelton and he were seated again.

"I think it's a wicked thing of the police," said the lady.

"They just hate the natives and any time they can humiliate them, they'll do it!"

Mr. Pendelton tried to soothe her. "But you must remember, my dear, that the man was quite within his rights. Jonah is an escaped prisoner, say what we like. Perhaps it would have been better if we had taken him in as soon as we got back. But who would have guessed that that monster, Balatwa, would have informed against Jonah? A man who is a menace to society! He's the one who should be behind bars, not Jonah!"

The three men sat talking over their plans for Jonah until the chimes of a nearby tower-clock chimed midnight.

"We can't have him languishing in prison; he'll get as bedraggled and dirty as he was the last time. Think we can arrange bail for him?"

"They'll set it pretty high," boomed the lawyer. "In the eyes of the law Jonah is still a murderer!"

"I'll ring up Alan Paton tomorrow," said the parson. "He's a friend of the African. Those books of his have won your race a lot of friends all over the world."

The two Africans nodded. "A very good man," said Mukalo.

"He is a good friend of a man who has a lot of influence at the court; it might help. But it's too late to phone tonight. We all need rest, too. I hope Jonah will sleep well," he added.

At the police station, the sergeant on duty towered over Jonah who was directly under a strong light. He and a detective began to question him. Their words came quick and hard – first one, then the other hurling questions and angry epithets at the youth.

The night was warm, and Jonah's brow began to run with perspiration. An hour before he had been soaring in bliss; now he was struggling in the quicksand of despair. He prayed desperately. *O God, help me!* But nothing seemed to stop the force or the flow of the men's words and accusations.

"Where have you been?"

"Who did you see?"

"Who financed you?"

"Did you have anything to do with that bombing?"

"That fire?"

"That theft?"

They hardly gave him a chance to answer their volley of questions. One of them slapped him with the back of his hand, sending a shower of inward sparks to his brain and making his ear ring. Then more slaps.

After a while Jonah got over his terror. He said with dignity, "If you'll only stop shouting I'll tell you everything. I did not want to escape. You know that very well. I did not murder the man who was killed. Those *tsotsis* got me away from the police van and Mr. Kwanda sent me into Rhodesia. What else could I do—?"

Another volley of vile curses drowned his explanation. A fiercer blow made his eyes water and nose begin to bleed. The words "nigger" and "kaffir" were used often, with obscenities in front of them.

Suddenly Jonah said, "God will punish you for this! I am going to be a minister of His, and He won't let anything really bad happen to me – outside His knowledge!"

The mouths of the White Policemen fell open in surprise. For a moment they stopped their abuse. Then one said, "Well, now. He's going to a minister! Can't you see him dolled up in a black suit and a white collar? Ha, ha!" The other joined in the laughter. Jonah hung his head, and his cheeks burned partly from shame and partly from the blows. But his words did some good. The men left him. Perhaps the mention of God had penetrated even their debased souls.

A White Policeman came in and led Jonah to a cell. He unlocked the door, pushed Jonah inside, took off his handcuffs, and went out, again locking the door. Jonah fell on his knees by the side of the rough bunk, and prayed as he had never prayed before.

17

JONAH'S HEAD WAS ONE BIG ACHE. He woke at the sound of the rattling of a key in the lock of his cell. A guard was there with a rough tin pan containing *sadsa*. He shoved it on the floor and went out again, locking the door. Jonah sat with his head resting on his hands; he did not feel like eating the *sadsa*. His life seemed to have fallen into pieces all around him; his hopes shattered. Worst of all, his white friends – to whom he had looked for deliverance – seemed powerless. What would happen to him? Was it worthwhile to think for a better way of life when there was so much hatred in the world? Then, like a faint echo of an answering voice when you are lost in the jungle, came the sound of the words of Psalm 31, read by Mr. Webster, in that dining room in Salisbury:

"Pull me out of the net that they have laid for me . . .
Deliver me from the hand of my enemies . . . ."

Jonah felt in his inner pocket. He had put an Easter leaflet there, one he had picked up in the church in Salisbury. Now the words came to him in that dismal cell like water in the desert. *I will not lose hope. Although my enemies seem so powerful – they snatched me right out of the home of the White Mfundisi – yet God is all-powerful and He will deliver me out of all trouble.*

It was about an hour later – ten o'clock – the guard said, "Come on!"

Jonah followed without a word. Their footsteps echoed loudly as they went through the corridors to the office. Jonah's heart gave a bound. There in the front office stood his three friends, Mr. Pendelton, Moses and Gideon. They were smiling. "You may go," said the official. "Here's your necktie and the things we took from you last night." He handed over an envelope and Jonah took it in a daze. He put on his tie automatically and brushed off his suit, sadly crumpled by his night in the cell. They walked out into God's sunshine. It was like a man getting out of hell.

"Oh, you're only out on bail, my boy," smiled Mr. Pendelton. "The means we've – that is, friends of yours – have put up a sum of money, as a guarantee that you won't run away again! I've been to see Mr. Paton, another fine friend, and he thinks he can get the trial brought forward – maybe next week. In the meantime, you're to stay with Moses, here, and help him decide what you'll say at the trial, and what witnesses we must bring to stand up for you!"

Jonah graspsed his friends' hands. "What it is to have friends!" he said. "I was almost in despair in that cell. And last night––" He felt his face. "They kept asking me questions; then they wouldn't wait for an answer––"

"By the way, did they strike you? Your face looks swollen to me!"

Jonah nooded. "It–it wasn't too bad! I suppose they thought I was stupid not to answer their questions the way they wanted."

The trio looked somber. "They're altogether too fond of beating up us Africans," boomed Mr. Mapomulo. "But try to get redress! They'll lie like Ananias if they are accused of trying the third degree on those arrested! It's this devilish hatred we're up against!"

"Well, thank God, you're out of that – for the time being, anyway," said Mr. Pendelton. "Here's my car. I'll take you to Mr. Mapomulo's. Keep up your courage and keep praying!"

18

IT WAS THE SAME COURTROOM. It all came back to Jonah in a nightmarish rush. In fact, the whole episode was like a bad dream, once dreamed, then uncomfortably remembered in the retelling. It was as though he had lived this bad moment already in his life and knew what was ahead. The room was crowded. It all looked the same as it had before. And again the whispers, like the buzzing of many bees. Jonah could not hear the words, only the buzzing; and he could see the excited pointing of fingers.

"That's the one, ain't it?"

"Yeah . . . the filthy Kaffir!"

"Imagine, using a gun on a White Man, why he ought to——"

"He's the one who escaped custody, eh? Well, they caught 'im again!"

"I hear he ain't guilty . . ."

"Rumor, is all. He's guilty all right, just look at 'im."

"I dunno. They say he was 'framed' with somebody else's gun . . . that another chap will be indicted."

"Hummph . . . news to me. I still think he's the one. Lookit . . . that Black . . . all dressed up like a White Man – collar and tie 'n all. If anyone deserves to die, it's him – show these Kaffirs they need to stay in their place."

Jonah heard none of this, of course. But based on two decades of life with these White People, he knew the gist of their comments and whispered conversations. And again the thought came to him. *Have I not already lived this even in my life? It is all the same. I remember it . . . but no – there is Tarzan, sitting at that table with the policeman. Before, he sat up here.* Jonah turned and craned his neck toward the gallery. It was filled with strange black faces.

He looked back at Tarzan who was now staring at him. The *tsotsi* leader did not seem so imposing in custody. But he angrily glared at Jonah as if to say, "One word too many from you and——" Jonah could imagine Tarzan's threatening gesture.

Jonah smiled back at Tarzan in a display of courage and imposing purpose. He was not frightened by the "General" any more.

"Constable Schultz!"

The second policeman told the same story as the first. Moses said he had no questions to put to this witness.

"Judas Balatwa!" Jonah's heart gave an involuntary jump. So Judas was back in town! And he was to be a witness! A witness against him – Jonah! Balatwa – the "Lieutenant" – dressed in his flashy clothes and wearing his golden smile, walked in his proud way to the witness box. Judas grinned at him; it made Jonah feel sick.

Mr. Pienaar picked up his papers and peered through his thick glasses at the man. "I understand you have been on a business trip to Rhodesia? You were a representative of *Africa Speaks?* Right?" Judas's smile was bigger than ever. He nodded.

"While in Salisbury you came across the accused. What was he doing?"

"Working at the place where they store the petrol, and where they dole it out to motorists!"

"And what did you find out about the accused? That he was engaged in subversive activities?" Jonah's heart went low in his body. What wickedness!

Judas nodded. "He is a very boastful man! I saw him in his room at the Location. He told me" – again it seemed everyone in that crowded room was holding his breath – "he only got work there so he could blow up the cans of petrol and oil!"

Jonah wanted to stand up and shout out "It's a lie!" but the lawyer caught him by the arm.

"You mustn't speak now! Later!"

Mr. Pienaar went across to the table and picked up "Exhibit B." He took out an egg-shaped thing. Everyone gasped. He held it up. "And is this one of the grenades – of Russian manufacture – that he showed to you? And that you *took from him?"* Jonah's whole soul seemed to freeze. To turn the thing around so that he was being accused for the crimes of Judas was the ultimate blow.

"You may question the witness!"

Moses stood up. He knew of Balatwa. Knew what an utter *skelm* he was; that he had made a living by scheming ever since he came to the Rand and would not stop at any crime. "No questions, your honor!" Jonah was crushed. Even Moses was not defending him.

"Nathan Kapazuni!" Moses started and Jonah felt the uneasy

feeling inside his heart increasing. Even Tarzan was being called as a witness! What did it mean!

A stir went through the court-room as the "General," a cheeky grin on his face, took the witness stand.

Mr. Pienaar adjusted his glasses, coughed, and said, "You are, I believe, serving a sentence as a 'found-in' at the plant of the *Africa Speaks*. Right?"

"Yes, but I didn't do——"

"Merely answer my questions. Do you know the accused?"

Tarzan looked across at Jonah with an evil grin. "Yes, he was a member of our club. We call ourselves 'the Russians'!"

"I see! And what happened on the night of the nineteenth?"

Jonah leaned forward, holding his breath. A hush fell over the courtroom. What would Tarzan say? For a moment a wild hope went through his heart that the "General" would confess that the whole gang went to rob the store, and that he, Jonah, refused to take part in the actual robbery.

"This man – er, the accused – wanted to rob the store of *Baas* Lipshotz, and we tried to stop him. He would not listen. He took my gun, and that's the last we saw of him until now!"

Jonah felt his blood run cold. What brazen lying! Surely the ground would open him and swallow him up. But no! Tarzan continued to swagger and grin. Jonah sprang to his feet, struggling to find words, but Moses dragged him down. "Don't say a word!" he hissed. "It will only make things worse!" Jonah sat in a daze. He looked around at the faces of the officials. The judge did not look shocked; Mr. Pienaar was smiling in a self-satisfied sort of way; the constables looked as though they believed Tarzan. What could he do against such a combination of evil?

"And then you saw by the paper that this man, Jonah Umlungu, had been arrested?"

Tarzan nodded, then spoke, "Yes, we read of his crime then."

"Any questions, 'Mr. Defense'?" Mr. Pienaar seemed to be enjoying himself. A satisfied smile was on his face. It was nice to see this upstart – this Kaffir who pretended to be a lawyer – made to look foolish.

Moses stood up. His deep voice boomed across the room, stilling the excited whispers of the crowd. "May we have 'Exhibit A,' please?"

He was handed a large envelope. Out of it he took Tarzan's

gun – the murder weapon. Again a buzz of noise filled the room and the judge banged his wooden hammer. Then silence fell.

Tarzan's mouth fell open. How had they found the gun? He did not think anyone would have thought of looking under the floor boards. Then an unpleasant thought went through his mind. He had wondered why Sergeant deVilliers had come into his cell and put black ink on his fingers, then pressed them on to a sheet of white paper. He thought it was just routine, taking fingerprints. Now he wondered! That gun must be full of his marks! Ah, but good old Judas had lied splendidly! And he had done his share. Surely, they would put all the blame on this stupid Jonah – the Hyena! His lawyer didn't know much. *I'll just stick to my story that Jonah had taken the gun from me on the night of the murder and I haven't seen it since.*

Moses' face was stern. His eyes seemed to bore right into those of Tarzan. "Do you recognize this gun?"

"It's mine. Or was, until this man took it from me the night the man was killed!"

A gasp of surprise went through the room. Someone laughed. The judge tapped his hammer again. It seemed strange that this swaggering witness would have given up his gun to the meek prisoner.

"No more questions!" Tarzan stepped down. His heart was glad. This stupid lawyer had taken his word that he had given the gun to Jonah.

Tarzan was taken back to the guard with whom he had been sitting. He settled back to enjoy the rest of the "show," and to laugh at the defeat of Jonah and his lawyer. *Oh, they wouldn't hang the stupid guy! It's his first crime and they'll realize he had only just come to the city and was green to all Goldie's ways. Still, he deserves a jolt; he is too fond of going around with the White Man, and dressing up to look like a somebody.*

"Have you any more witnesses?" The judge looked at Mr. Pienaar.

The prosecutor adjusted his glasses on his nose, peered out and then shuffled his papers.

"I think that's all, your honor!"

The judge rose. "Then we'll adjourn until two o'clock this afternoon."

Jonah, feeling sick at heart, followed Mr. Mapomulo into the office where the lawyers gathered. Everything had gone wrong! What could a person do against such a torrent of lies and the hatred of the

White officials? They had already passed sentence upon him. He sat in a chair and buried his face in his hands. Moses patted him on the shoulder. "Don't give way to despair, my friend," he said. "It's not over yet!" Jonah groaned.

The door opened. Mr. Pendelton and Gideon came in. The Rector's face was pink with indignation. "What colossal liars! Did you ever hear anything like it? Twisting the evidence to make their vileness apply to Jonah! Surely the judge will see through their deceit?"

Again the door opened, and a firm hand was laid on Jonah's shoulder. He looked up. "Mfundisi Beckwith!" He jumped to his feet and grasped the hand of his old mission-settlement pastor.

"I just got here in time for the trial, Jonah," he said. His kind eyes brought cheer to Jonah's heart. "I heard all the lying evidence of those scoundrels. All we can do now is to pray! Don't give up, Jonah! Your lawyer here will stand by you!"

"Things look pretty black, Moses," said Mr. Pendelton, seating himself. "What is our next step?"

All eyes were on the African lawyer. His face was grave. He knew what he was up against. If Jonah had been a White Man, and he a White Lawyer, all would have been well. But when even the Black witnesses turned against their own race, and the hatred and prejudice of the Whites was brought to bear on his client, things looked hopeless.

"We've got one more string to our bow," he said quietly. "Apart, of course, from the help of God. The fingerprints on the gun. If they are not Jonah's and are found to be those of Tarzan, I don't see what else they can do but exonerate Jonah here."

"They've taken your fingerprints, haven't they, Jonah?"

Jonah nodded.

"Sergeant DeVilliers wouldn't take fingerprints off the gun at first," said Moses. "He said they had proved by the bullets that it was the murder weapon all right, but that there was no need to see who had handled the gun last. As you know, Mr. Pendelton, it took all your persuasion, and your friends' to get him to take the prints and compare them to Tarzan's!"

"But he did do it eventually?"

"I think so! But he wouldn't give me the satisfaction of knowing for sure!"

"You'll call him as a witness, of course?"

"Yes, but will he admit the truth? They hate me so much because I'm Black, and have no right to know the law . . . and they hate to admit that they've been wrong about Jonah. He might even go as far as to lie under oath!"

"Oh no! Surely not!" His audience looked at him.

"It has been done!"

A timid knock. Someone opened the door and there stood Miriam. Her lovely face was tense with worry and fear. Jonah had not seen her in the courtroom, although he thought she might be there. Their eyes met again in a hurried look of love. "What do you want, Miriam?" said Mr. Pendelton kindly.

The girl found it difficult to speak, but at last stammered; "I haven't said anything before, because – because – he said he'd kill me——"

"Who? What are you talking about?" asked the Rector.

"Tarzan!" She paused, as though she might not want to speak. Then it came out in a rush! "I saw him hide the gun!"

"You *saw* him?"

She nodded, her breath coming in quick gasps. "I did not know it was a gun he was hiding. All I know is I came suddenly to his room to clean up – the morning after the murder – and he didn't hear me. He was stooping down by the bed and I heard a noise like the board in the floor had been moved. But it was the way he acted that made me wonder about him. Not at the time, but later. His face was full of anger. He came at me as though he would kill me. 'If you tell what you saw, I'll do you in,' he said, and he meant it! Now I think it over, I'm sure he was hiding the gun under the floor!"

She stopped, and sank into a chair Mr. Beckwith placed for her.

"And you would go into the witness box?" asked the pastor.

Her face showed the pain of the very worst kind of fear. "I–I'd hate to, but – if I could do anything to save Jonah, I'd do it!"

Jonah's heart began slowly to lift. Perhaps things were not so bad after all. He would pray more, and believe. This despair was dishonoring to God and his faith.

"You must all come to my place for lunch," said the pastor. "We've some time before the afternoon session." They gladly piled into his car and drove to the manse. Mrs. Pendelton had expected some such emergency and was glad to welcome them at her roomy table. After the meal the minister read the story of Peter's release from prison – "all because his friends had prayed for him" he added, "and offered prayer that God would intervene and cause truth to triumph."

Many more people crowded into the courtroom. Their eyes shone with excitement. This was better than the theater. This was real life drama! They had been annoyed when the judge put off the climax of the mystery story, but it was sure to come this afternoon. They spoke in loud whispers of all that had taken place that morning.

"Oh, he's as good as hanged."

"He doesn't stand a chance."

"Not with that mad Kaffir lawyer!"

One or two stood up for Jonah. "I like that boy's face," said a woman, "and I certainly don't like the looks of that Balatwa, or that – what did they call him? – Kapazuni. Bad eggs, if you ask me!"

The clerk got up and rhymed off the same string of words he had recited in the morning. "Everybody rise!" All stood and amid the same awesome silence Judge Elliott walked in, his long black gown swinging in the breeze made by his entry, and his white curled wig adding an extra air of dignity to his thin, thoughtful face.

He had been thinking a lot in the recess about the evidence Mr. Pienaar had brought forth in the morning session and he did not like it. *It's hard for me to believe that a Zulu from the country – only lately come to the Rand – should be capable of making a confirmed tsotsi part with his gun, seeing it was the only one the gang possessed.* He had not been impressed by the appearance of Judas Balatwa. He had always liked Moses Mapomulo and had encouraged him in cases he had conducted before this one. But he must be strictly impartial. He must not allow his natural leanings toward one side to cause him to err in judgment. He sensed the hatred of the Afrikaners toward the natives, and he had long and unsuccessfully fought against it.

"Order! The court is in session!"

The judge looked down at Mr. Mapomulo. "I believe you were examining your witnesses. Have you any more before we have the summing up of the case? Perhaps it would be better to have the scribe read out the account of the proceedings before we begin, so as to refresh our minds."

Ah, I know it all too well! thought Jonah.

The clerk read from his shorthand notes. He had faithfully set down every word that anyone had said. There it was, in black and white – Balatwa's awful lies about Jonah in Salisbury and Tarzan's lies about the gun. The two constables' stilted words – all there. And would be until the archives crumbled to dust. Still, his heart was not nearly as numb as it had been before the recess. The thought of Miriam, flushed and bright-eyed, thinking enough of him to conquer her fear to witness for him; it was wonderful. And Mfundisi Beckwith coming all the way from Zululand to be present at his trial! And the faith of his other two minister friends. It was wonderful to think he had friends who would believe in him, and stand by him whatever happened.

"Sergeant DeVilliers!"

Again a murmur rustled over the crowd. Sergeant DeVilliers, of the C.I.D.? What did he have to do with the case? The gavel ended their whispers.

The sergeant came in, a look of annoyance on his face. He hated appearing in a case in which a Kaffir was concerned, unless it was to say something that would send him to the cells – or better yet, the gallows! He hated to admit he had been wrong about the fingerprints, but there was no mistake. The prints on the gun that Moses Mapomulo handed him were definitely those of Tarzan – Nathan Kapazuni. If he could get out of admitting it he would.

Moses fixed his dark, melancholy eyes on the pale blue shifty eyes of the sergeant. "Sergeant DeVilliers, you are attached to the fingerprint department in the C.I.D., I believe?"

"You know I am!"

The judge spoke up. "Answer the questions Mr. Mapomulo asks you – without comment!"

The sergeant looked angrier than ever.

"Do you remember that, on the twenty-ninth I handed you a gun, purporting to belong to the witness, Nathan Kapazuni, and to have come from his room at the plant of *Africa Speaks?"*

"Yes!" It was the shortest, sharpest way he could say it.

Moses paused before asking the next question. Jonah, and all his friends present, sent up a silent prayer that the man would tell the truth.

"Sergeant," the lawyer's deep voice was lower and deeper than ever. Its very solemnity brought an end to the tense whisperings. "You tested the gun for fingerprints?"

"Yes!"

The silence was so silent that the noise of the honking of traffic outside the court came in clearly. "Now, I want you to tell the court whose fingerprints you found on the gun. Were they those of the accused?"

DeVilliers thought hard. How he'd like to say they were. But he was afraid there'd be an investigation and perhaps that promotion to staff sergeant would not come through.

"No!"

"Then whose were they——?"

"Objection!" Mr. Pienaar was on his feet.

Moses stopped, flustered.

"What objection?"

"The question is irrelevant and immaterial! You have proved they were not those of the defendant, that is enough!"

Anyone could see that Mr. Pienaar was angry because the case was not going in the way he wanted it to, and he was trying to save face.

"Objection overruled!" Judge Elliott's voice was sharp. "Now, Sergeant, tell us whose fingerprints they were." Tarzan's face, with all its dark hue, was turning different colors. His plans to make this stupid country boy take the blame had backfired. His cowardly heart started beating fast; he knew he was doomed. He looked around, his eyes darting from window to door. He jumped up and started to run, but the guard was too quick for him. He seized Tarzan by the collar, and sat him down hard.

"That's the man!" said the sergeant, reluctantly. "The one they call Tarzan!"

The judge's wooden mallet could not stop the hub-bub that filled the courtroom. Moses clapped his client on the shoulder. Jonah felt as though stars were shooting across his brain. It was a miracle! He had been cleared – at least on the charge of murder. He looked up and caught sight of Miriam amidst the crowd. She had not needed to testify after all! Their eyes met, and Jonah's heart gave a great throb of joy.

"Nathan Kapazuni, stand up!" Tarzan was actually crying! Great tears rolled down his flabby cheeks. Like most bullies he was a coward at heart.

"Nathan Kapazuni," the judge's voice was stern. "You are accused of the murder of Jacob Lipshotz. Date of trial to be decided later. Take him back to his cell, guard!"

There was silence while Tarzan, a pitiful, cowed object, shuffled out. When the door closed, the judge said: "I think you will agree, Mr. Pienaar, that there is no need of a summing up of the evidence. It seems plain the accused is not guilty – indeed, could not have killed the merchant because he never had use of the gun."

"However," the judge continued, "stand up, Jonah Umlungu.

As you were with the gang, as you admit, on the night the crime was committed . . . although I believe you had no intentions of taking part in the robbery, and did not enter the store, you were in bad company."

Jonah held his breath and looked into the face of the judge. "Therefore, I sentence you to six months in the penitentiary" – a collective gasp went up; Jonah's spirits went down–"sentence suspended conditional on your good behavior and upon your reporting to the Reverend Michael Pendelton every week for a year!"

The judge tried to keep his face stern, but he could not repress a smile when he saw the look on Jonah's face. The youth's eyes were big with amazement and joy.

"Case dismissed!"

19

"IT IS NOT GENERALLY SUNG at weddings," said the Reverend Gideon Mukalo, as he stood, hymn book in hand, at the front of the little frame church. "But I think the bridegroom feels it most appropriate – especially one of the verses!"

Mr. Beckwith, who was performing the ceremony jointly with the African minister, looked slightly puzzled at the change in procedure. But Jonah smiled. He had asked to have the words read as part of the ceremony:

"Jesus shall reign where'er the sun
Doth his successive journeys run;
His Kingdom stretch from shore to shore
Till suns shall rise and set no more."

The little church was packed with Africans – the women on one side and the men on the other, according to custom. After the reading of the words of the hymn, Reverend Mukalo invited the congregation to sing it. The building soon rang with the voices of African Christians lifting praises to God and singing of the final triumph of their Saviour.

Miriam stood beside Jonah, her hand held tightly in his. The eyes of both were misty with love and reverence for the moment. The bride was radiant in a lovely white wedding dress and bouquet of wild African flowers from the veld. Jonah, in a dark suit, listened attentively to the words of the two ministers.

In the back of his mind the words of the hymn still echoed:

"Where He displays His healing power
Sin and the Curse are known no more . . . ."

Yes, the Curse had gone forever! No more would he have to blame his fate when things went wrong.

"God has ordained the institution of matrimony and hallowed it . . ." Jonah was listening to the words of Reverend Mukalo, yet was able to follow his own thoughts as well. ". . . and these two before you today understand well the hand of God in their lives."

Yes! Jonah wanted to shout how true that was, but propriety and reverence for the moment limited his reaction to a slight nod of agreement. He had seen enough of the good hand of God to realize that His power was stronger than that of the world of evil, of black magic, strong as that was.

"Jonah and Miriam have both given their lives, their talents, their all to the Saviour. In this holy act of marriage these two desire to unite as one in a common love for each other and for the Saviour, to serve one another and in turn be servants of Christ is their desire. And so we are here to consecrate these vows to God, to husband and to wife."

Here he was, about to become the husband of Miriam! It was too much – like a dream. But no, there is a difference between dreams and reality. This was most real.

"Miriam . . . do you take this man, Jonah . . . ."

He had had a long talk with Mr. Pendelton after his release from the nightmares of court and subsequent actions. Now it was all behind him and there was no reason why he should put off his marriage to Miriam.

"I will . . ." The voice was that of the girl, soft and yet decisive.

The minister turned to Jonah, smiling, and repeated the vows. "I will," echoed the groom.

The minister was concluding the ceremony. Jonah's full attention was given to his remarks and to the words of his prayer for the couple. He finished and asked them to stand. "May I present my good friends and choice servants of God, Mr. and Mrs. Jonah Umlungu!"

The small, almost antique, organ began to play. All the stops were pulled and the bride and groom strode quickly down the aisle to stand at the back of the small church in a receiving line.

During the reception Jonah rose to speak. The nearly fifty guests hushed and listened. Eyes dark, clear, shining, Jonah told them of his and Miriam's plans and of their gratitude for the many Christian favors. He looked like the student he would soon be. "Night school will take up our evenings. Both Miriam and I will be attending. She will stay on as domestic for the good Reverend Pendelton and I will serve as his gardener. They are most kind to help us in this way."

Then his ebony features grew serious. "A few weeks ago, as you know, I was a poor African, groaning underneath the weight of a stupid Curse." His dark eyes seemed to seek out everyone in the small room while Miriam's eyes were fixed proudly on her new husband. Jonah flung his arms out to emphasize a point. "Now, I am free! God has led me through many strange paths. The world is much the same – the City and the veld – both lead to wrong. There is but one true path."

He paused. "We long for *Uhuru* and want the day to hurry when our people will be free. But we can be free even though oppressed. We can be free in the Saviour. It was in this strange country that I found Christ. And I – that is, we –" and he smiled to Miriam – "mean to serve Him faithfully the rest of our days."